Notes for a Young Gentleman

Notes for a Young Gentleman

TOBY LITT

LONDON NEW YORK CALCUTTA

Seagull Books, 2018

© Toby Litt, 2018

ISBN 978 0 8574 2 485 3

British Library Cataloguing-in-Publication Data
A catalogue record for this book is available from the British Library.

Typeset in Dante MT Regular by Seagull Books, Calcutta, India
Printed and bound by Maple Press, York, Pennsylvania, USA

Until you have read this through, do not write in it. If you choose to do so thereafter, that is your own mistake.

It was spooked England, all laid out below and invisibly rushing up towards one—thirty-two feet per second per second—and how intimately I knew it and how passionately I loved it; as I fell, as I fell; once again.

. . the foxes refurbishing the entrance to their den—laying decoy trails for the hounds who will come again soon; . . .

. . the buck with its purposeful halt and the mortal chal-
lenge of its red gaze; . . .

. . the stoats performing their deeds because, as stoats,
they are more than capable of deeds; . . .

. . the coddled husband-cat stepping out for further
screwing whilst yesterday's farm-kittens lie crisping in
hessian; . . .

. . the tea-cosy dormouse so adorably a-snuggle beneath
the floorboards of the abandoned cottage; . . .

. . the hisp of the bat, too high-pitched for lettering, halfway between the eave and the oak branch, doubling back on its doublings-back; . . .

. . the increased air-pressure beneath the barn owl's wings, oppressing the field-mouse, forcing it down the stalk and into the purple-thick of the wheat; . . .

. . the starlings spread out like stars, covered in stars, beneath the invisible stars; . . .

. . sparrows who take their own wings as the best blankets, dipping their heads into the blacked-out warm-shadows; sparrows, disbelieving of how slowly their hearts are beating, even though ready for immediate flight; . . .

. . moles who are there but who do not deign to emerge, unless for dangerous gossip; . . .

. . the dead badger, rotting like Sodom and Gomorrah beneath the ivy whence in its last exercise of good judgement it had betaken itself to die; . . .

. . the ivy as emblem of its own tenacity, a shelter for the spider's young.

Lovely England—long johns and empty breadbins; servants' quarters and two of gold-top, please; conkers in murky vinegar and sprained ankle at the village fête; green grass and don't strike too sudden if you want to catch the tench; also.

Of all the unnatural, nonsensical things a human being can do, jumping from an aeroplane at ten thousand feet is probably the most exhilarating; spin.

This gorgeous night was far too succulently dark to do something as stupid as parachuting, and yet somehow one found oneself parachuting.

A sealed-dove: Jumping out of the plane itself was like finally speaking one's love to the object of one's obsession; terror.

With one's love, though, there is always the possibility one will be lifted to higher heights; with a parachute jump, the only exhilaration is the acceleration of one's failure.

It is awfully hard not to feel—classic—that to fall is to fail; even if one is doing it pretty well.

The first of my astonishments was the acceleration, then the simple fact that I was moving towards the earth in a way that would kill me if I did nothing about it.

By the time one has realized what one is actually doing, one realizes one no longer has time in which to do anything but survive.

Upside-down world: My previous runs had been dry, and now the uprushing air felt like the plunging waters of a waterfall.

The new moon was no moon, sickle-hidden from the earth behind chinkless clouds—clouds out of which one had just tumbled.

Although one knew there must be a difference in quality between the blackness of the woods and the blackness of the cornfields, one could not for the life of one make it out. Not from this height.

And my confusion wasn't helped by the hushing-howling air-rush in my ears, or the shivers which had started to convulse my body.

One feels abysmally safe—the whole sensation-of-fall being so classically dreamlike that one knows death will only mean awaking with a cosy bang back in bed.

The iron sea was all behind one now; one might—if one were unlucky—land in water, in the ornamental lake, but would have a chance to outswim drowning; as long as the canopy didn't fall directly on top of one.

How could I have lived in this world so long and yet never before have seen it?

Seen from directly above, the pylons look like spider webs—when and if said webs are exposed by moon-light.

The rivers Northwards glossed over themselves, still stilling, comparable to nothing but cold molten mirrors.

This world abstractly is too full of worlds beautifully for one person comprehensively to dwell in it desperately.

I was almost too overcome by thoughts of my homeland to remember that I would die if I didn't remember to open my parachute. The instrument to achieve this was still grasped in my fist. Of course, at the first glimpse of tree-shaped darknesses beneath, I had stopped counting. Any idea of time-keeping was in the realms of the bizarre. Probably I had been in sight of the dark-that-wasn't-clouds for ten or fifteen or twenty. Time to slow myself down—and when I realized that the way to prolong this imaginary view was to pull the cord, I did so immediately.

The black silk puckers above me, threatening to fold, and then with a colossal whump it goes resplendent into full black-swan mode.

Whump—a surprise even despite having practised the whole routine once a night for an entire week.

The canopy open above my head is, now I have done what I should and checked it, fine—the black of it has been turned almost indigo by the occluded moonlight.

I am not a soldier, and I do not intend to express myself like one. I believe I am a gentleman. Even at moments of pain and peril, and of them there are to be plenty, there is beauty here to be noted and later turned into phrases.

Winston Churchill, obviously—there could be no other target; glider, not plane.

The crows sitting blackly smug in the middle of their murder—even when on the edge, they know they are in the middle: when they fly, as they do not now, it is in a tumble of overtaking and falling back.

But perhaps after all I should have been paying more attention to where I was heading—the air wasn't pushing me, but sideways and very fast was the direction I seemed to be going.

I hadn't realized quite how still the night had been until suddenly it ceased to be so.

Still several hundred feet from the ground, I feel a flash of sudden wind go past my face. I have no idea what it might have been—no bird travels that fast, or is that big, or disappears that absolutely.

I glanced upwards, a moment later, and I seemed to see a shadow being projected upon the black silk of the parachute by something intervening between it and the white sliver of the moon—an oddly triangular shape, if it came from a small, stray, lower cloud.

But there is no time for speculation; not even when the something seems to brush against the top of the canopy and give out a cry that sounds almost like sexual climax.

The wind blowing past me was perfumed with scents of flowers I hadn't smelled for years, and should not have been smelling then—cedarwood, chrysanthe-mums; why should their scent be up here? My experi-ence of parachuting was so very limited—perhaps these high-in-the-air sensations of scent and shadow were a commonly observed phenomenon.

I felt something until some time later quite incomprehensible—the wind seeming not to push me but, at first, to circle around me. At the same time, the clouds directly above opened themselves, quite as if commanded to—I suspected this, slightly, even at the time, falling. Was I entering into the top of the least likely tornado or whirlwind? Our county, that I knew, had never known one.

The canopy, black silk, appears now like some moon jellyfish; I know that if it had been made of white it would be many times brighter, but still it seems to be sticky with moonbeams—as if they aren't reflected from its surface but remain there, aglow, attached, alive.

If I attracted attention as I fell, things would become very difficult for me upon the ground. I am something that should be nailed to a tree and left there, as a warning to others.

Of all things, apart from plummeting direct to my death, I had hoped to at least make it to the earth without initiating a pursuit.

The hounds, jowl to heel and tail to flank, in their luxurious kennel; whimpering out their dreams of pursuit through trees, through water; chuffing their teeth into future bodies.

The tugging wind for a moment stills—I am scheduled to land in the High Field, alongside but not too close to the thick eldritch wood known as The Darkenings.

After this, I would descend Crackback Hill and begin my mission.

At least now I can make out the elongated wedge of dense woodland that is my ambition, after hopefully surviving the landing.

The breeze, however, seems to have other notions. It is pushing and pushing me in the direction of The House Beautiful, my ancestral domain. I will be going here soon enough, but to be impaled on the weather vane would not serve my cause, or that of dear old Adolf Hitler.

Still, the undear old place looked gorgeous from this angle—a hope of this view had been one of my reasons for attempting the mission. Also, the chance to burn the whole shebang to the ground (this was permitted, but only after the primary objective had definitely been achieved).

Perhaps, indeed, I should still be paying more attention to where I am heading.

I needed a plan; I had a plan; I needed a plan.

Lower down, halfway between the clouds and the ground, the wind was racing sideways, Eastwards, seeming to wish to suck me into The Darkenings.

My instructors, Jens and Jurgen, had warned me repeat-edly of the dangers of landing anywhere other than open ground. They had put on a jolly Kraut slideshow of broken necks—of dark shapes lodged in upper branches, of twisted puppets hanging from chimney-stacks, and even one unlucky sausage who had fallen straight down a village well. What perplexed me most was that the photographs all seemed to betray the same style—as if one particular artist had been on hand minutes after each of these mishaps, suggesting they hadn't been mishaps at all.

I could feel my escaped fringe bashing into the corners of my eyes, another thing I'd been warned about. Yet still I had rejected offers of a Germanic haircut.

In fact, I was behind two months' growth of unwashed beard—a tramp was what I intended to appear, brassy-burnished with old dirt. A gentleman of the highway, besotted by beer, unfit for serving my country, likely to steal any weapon, likely to piss in any bed . . .

To come down in thick woodland would be a total gamble (with my life, if that counts), the odds definitely stacked towards me ending up with a snapped neck—either that or stuck up a tree for the next glory-seeking Home Guardsman to come along and arrest/bayonet. My orders, in such circumstances, were explicit: I was to crunch and swallow the cyanide capsule sewn into my collar. And if it looked at any point that my mission had failed, or that I was likely to be captured, that was exactly what I intended to do. I was not going to allow myself to be caught—the very idea of watching my grandfather as he safely came to visit me, up a tree!

In the last fifty yards, I was pushed at least half that distance sideways; Western winds, blowing now.

The scent of flowers became stronger and stronger as I came closer to the ground.

But it was trees I was really heading for—a very large oak that, from one second to the next, turned itself from just another beautiful tree into my life-or-death fate.

It is ten yards, five.

I covered my eyes—to try, at least, to save them.

I could feel my legs shattering, even though they had yet to touch down. I could feel them as they would shatter.

And then I was into the tree, still falling—I could feel it surrounding me, like a cloud, but I had yet to touch it.

Then the strings around me all of a sudden tighten, tighten, and a great downwards thrust goes through me.

My chin fell against my chest and I could feel all my teeth, individually.

The helmet, which had never fitted me properly, slipped forwards over my face, cutting into the bridge of my nose.

My feet seemed to tug down on the rest of my body, as if there were another person hanging from them.

And then, just as suddenly but twice as sillily, I am travelling upwards—the fall converted into a bounce; O trampoline!

I feel the strings go slack as I rise, seemingly in slow-motion, their black lines going wiggly, and then again I fall. A few more juddery bounces, and I come to a swaying stop—leaf-bowered—and am able to take a proper look around.

A gentleman should arrive at his destination, after however arduous a journey, quite as if he had just taken a turn around the rose garden.

Instantly, I realized I knew this tree; it was the tallest this side of The Darkenings. I had even climbed it before, higher than this height—for I found myself suspended, dangling, in the very heart of the tree. It was still another twenty to twenty-five feet approximately to the ground.

When I took a proper look up, I saw the canopy had spread itself out as a black cap over the treetop.

The strings were drawn very tight, but—having not snapped already—they would (presumably) hold me for as long as I cared to stay there. The image of a puppet is, at this point, hard to avoid.

I had known there was a chance of this—there were three oaks in the High Field I had been briefed to avoid but might have hit—just as there had been a chance my parachute would fail to open.

I had already caused myself enough problems by allowing myself to be blown in this direction.

The real fault had come higher up, though, when I should have concentrated on my trajectory instead of becoming enraptured by the landscape.

I couldn't blame the pilot, Ludwig, or the navigator, Wolfgang—they could not have known of the cross-winds further down.

It wasn't really a decision—get down, get away from the tree. It wasn't really words.

One meets the Führer long before one is in his presence, and one feels the contact of him long after he is gone from one.

The plan had been for me to gather my parachute together, once I had landed, and then fold it up as neatly and bury it as deeply as I could. To leave it where it now was—well, it seemed like my entire mission had already failed. Cyanide, here I come.

I might have to head straight for the Norfolk coast, and the rendezvous point with the U-boat.

If come morning I was still beneath the tree, with its great advertisement of black silk, my capture would be only a matter of minutes.

Even now, so deep into the night, I couldn't be certain I hadn't been sighted already; my grandfather is insomniac, smokes, looks out of windows into the dark.

Fast action was needed; each moment I hung there was more perilous than the last.

I tried pulling myself up—that didn't work; the strings were too silken for me to gain any purchase.

Above me, the black dome of my parachute was draped over the arcing top of the oak tree quite as if the one had been designed to fit the other.

For a couple of minutes, I try to kick my legs back and forth, to exaggerate my sway into a swing. This works to an extent, but I never come close enough to an upper branch to grab it. I have been perfectly positioned for helplessness.

There is only one possible way down: the hard way.

One passed through many imposing doors and along many exposing corridors in one's long progress towards the Führer.

In my left breast pocket, for this exact reason, was my old faithful Swiss Army penknife—Swiss but not neutral; not in this conflict.

I glanced downwards, past my telescoping legs, my dangling boots. The main trunk of the tree did not interpose between myself and the ground.

Tree-climbing—I found it hard to believe this was once my greatest pleasure; aspired once. Tree-climbing without tree-climbing.

It amused me that I was technically in England but had yet to touch English soil.

A portrait of the Führer as high and wide as a two-up two-down house dominated the ante-room. In comparison to this, any human being would have appeared dwarven—and so one was adjusted to the shock of his being of human dimensions.

I was a dangling man, not for the last time.

All I could do, now, was cut the strings and pray for an injury-free, death-free drop.

There was a brass bust of the Führer, bulking, noble, which one was directed to inspect—implicitly encouraged to touch—and this was done in the knowledge that many, particularly women, would otherwise wish to

touch the Führer, just to prove to themselves his physical existence. The nose of this brass is rubbed to gold,
and will eventually wear away.

Some leaves had been caught beneath my harness. I
pulled one to rub against my cheek—it was inhumanly
cold, and I found that delightful.

My knife was ready for using.

> Many, upon first meeting the Führer, are wont to dis-
> grace themselves, and embarrass or distract him.

> Reports were legion of Generals, upon encountering
> the Führer, soiling their undergarments, at front or back
> or both, or middle-aged matrons abruptly attempting to
> breastfeed him.

With each string cut, I fell lower and lower—and began
to hope that, in this manner, I might descend at least
half the rest of the way.

> The ante-rooms, therefore, had been psychologically
> designed so as to forestall the worst of these undesirable
> intimacies.

> The doors opened; I was to be admitted—this was the
> moment.

But with a great series of pings, the last dozen strings
snapped in series and I was falling.

> The Führer was seated behind his very large desk when
> I entered his very large office.

To walk towards him, over silent-making carpets of thick-woven swastika pattern, took two minutes.

The light in the room is burnished. The light-sources are few—the desk lamp, some uplighters—it is the reflections from gilded surfaces which gives it its warmth, humour.

Albert Speer had done his work—even as one analysed the stage management, one was overawed by the stage management; everything was so positioned that the Führer himself, placed at the vanishing point, balancing the perspective, flanked by tall columns and guarded by his most loyal troops—the Führer could have been Chaplin's Little Tramp and it would have made no difference whatsoever, one would still have offered him the Heil Hitler salute.

I was falling and falling and falling.

As it was, as I approached, the Führer turned out to be addressing himself to some plans; I am not sure whether they were truly occupying his attention or if he was merely using them as an excuse to contemplate his world-destiny.

Of course, as a British serviceman, armed, I was not allowed unaccompanied into the Führer's presence.

Even though I was being entrusted with a top-secret mission costing many thousands of Reichsmarks, who knew what patriotic instincts might overtake me, given the chance to make an assassination?

Yet I must say, I have never in all my life felt so truly English as I did when taking those final few steps towards Hitler. He provided nationalism with absolute clarity; even when it wasn't his own.

Surely, this is what Winston Churchill and the British Army wants me to do? Surely this is my mission? Pretend to be loyal; get close to Hitler; kill him with your knife.

I might be able to do it, I thought. If I get close enough—away from the guards. Death as death.

Ten feet away—the opening of our conversation was predictable enough. "Heil Hitler," he replied.

I was waiting for him to look up—waiting to encounter that famous gaze—the all-penetrating stare that came also with Picasso.

How much power is to be gained over the world by looking at it in such a way that it believes you really see it—see it more clearly and more deeply than anyone has ever done before?

Falling and homing; ghost-words.

The Führer glanced up.

All emperors reward terrifyingly just as all emperors punish delightfully.

Those eyes, indescribable—although of course everyone tries to describe those eyes.

Even forewarned by legend and news reports, documentaries and biographies, nothing could have prepared me for the mild ferocity of the Führer's gaze.

Yet this was something I had never known before, even with my grandfather; it was a ferocity of total approval.

I was hoping to kill him, on behalf of the world. He seemed to despise the whole world, on my behalf, for not recognizing my true worth—a worth apparent only to myself and to him.

This must have won over so many, this gaze—why bother resisting? Why not go along with him, just to see what happens? My own will is pitiful, in comparison. I only exist as a crowd to be swayed. Let us follow. It will be worth it just to see what magnificent catastrophe follows. It will be worth it just to learn how an entity like this deals with failure. And if it succeeds, this giddiness, this glee, and I have been a supporter, there will be rewards.

"You are he," he said, in English, and then repeated himself in German. "You are he—Sie sind er."

This is not the voice of the radio broadcasts; it is far more seductive, playful.

When he comes closer—five feet away, four—eyes still looking, looking, one feels the very gaze of History upon one.

One knows this man to be Napoleon, to be Alexander, to be Hannibal, to be Julius Caesar—and yet for these instants of his epochal existence, I am all that seems ever to have existed for him.

He came forwards and reached out to me, swaying as he did so. Will he stumble?

I can smell his breath: gingery biscuity.

Before I can prepare myself I see his hand reaching out towards me—towards my face!

He was going to touch my face.

Why was Hitler going to touch my face?

He seems to want to touch our face.

What does he want to touch our faces for?

What does Hitler want with our faces?

You can remember it, can't you?

What is wrong with our faces? Are we bleeding? Or beautiful? Or about to die?

Beauty is youth willingly submitting itself to new forms of self-discipline.

These questions still resonate within us, in the present time; sender.

But Hitler doesn't, after all, touch my face; he puts his hand softly on my shoulder, only grazing my neck slightly with his thumbnail. Still to this day I can feel the line it traced.

There are scars we carry beneath our skins; not always proudly.

"You will do this," he said.

"For Germany," he said.

"For me," he said.

Now was the knife's moment.

I found I could do nothing but say the script pat, "Heil Hitler!" Even the actions, even the silly salute, even the heels.

What unmanned me quite was the Führer's own emotion at this moment—the fathomless depths to which he had been moved by me, by my presence.

His capacity to be affected was so profound as to be inhuman.

How could I have thought of anyone but Jesus Christ?

"Thank you," he said, sincerely—"Vielen Dank!"—as if I, personally, uniquely, had renewed his sense of mission.

He had entrusted me with the gift of a glimpse of his weakness. How he felt about how he felt. He needed others. He needed the world. He needed me.

Someone else touched my arm, although at that moment I would have sworn that the only two beings in existence were Adolf Hitler and myself.

That moment—it has lasted ever since, privileged even among all the other everlasting moments.

Admissions of weakness come from positions of strength.

"For Germany," by which he had meant "For Europe"—
the Europe that Germany, in its essence, has always rep-
resented; the West, not the East; the North, not the
South; the subtle, not the primitive; the rational, not the
dark; the principled, not the pragmatic; the pure, not
the besmirched. I was inside the words he had spoken,
admiring them like a cathedral. I could almost see how
this might become my religion.

The knife.

I had seen what was coming, and I wanted to tell him—I
was almost exploding with the words, "Don't make
Napoleon's mistake! Don't march on Moscow! Don't go
by winter!"

It was, I thought, in my power to change history, but I
could not. At this moment, I was a body-passenger.

The words were not allowed out of my mouth; the
knife would not leave my pocket.

He then said other words to me, or I have come to
remember him as saying other words to me.

"Go to England. Parachute into enemy territory.

"Observe nature. Observe the natural world of
England.

"Write a *lyrisches* poem in the German Romantic tradition. Goethe. Holderlin.

"Make your escape, and return to deliver the poem to
me.

"If we can steal a single true poem from the Britons, they will inevitably be defeated.

"Kill anyone who impedes you."

Clearly not. Clearly this is not something he said, but this is how I am starting to remember it—

A gentleman should never acknowledge a mere fact.

After such intimacy, one felt the only appropriate form of communication would have been singing—but this became, instead, a gentle mutual hum; for about five seconds Adolf Hitler and I hummed, as if trying to find each other's resonant frequencies.

The Führer then began to sing, not as one might have expected in the Wagnerian style, but in the manner of the Italianate Mozart. I took this to mean that he was content.

This was a moment beyond the clumsy grasp of doubt.

If only I could have prostrated myself.

If only I could have brought myself to kill him—but then everything that comes after would have been different, or not happened at all.

If only I could have allowed myself to say, "There is no God and you are doing His work."

I am a rentable nightingale. I eat your seed; I'll sing your song.

I loved him not for what he was, but for what he was giving me the chance to do: Kill my grandfather.

And even though I knew thousands of others had felt the same (the eyes, the eyes), and even though I knew I was part of a production-line of Führer-epiphanies, even though it was as mass-produced a thing as one of Henry Ford's hateful automobiles—still it worked on me—still this moment was mine—and still he was there and I was there and it was then and we were alone together.

I forgave him his Fordism, for I recognized it as a historical necessity: How else was he to do his work in the world?

Such as he cannot dawdle; they must meet us, inspire us and then turn away as we are ripped, shouting, from them. For of course we wish to cling: I would have exchanged my entire existence for that of a fleck of dandruff on the Führer's collar (I saw numerous).

Having seen so many actors playing Hitler, it was difficult not to end up comparing him to them rather than them to him. What I think none of the portrayals managed to capture was the man's conviction in his own silly destiny. Also, there was a fastidiousness to his movements which recalled the physical poetry of Chaplin's Great Dictator.

One never knows whom one has met until after one has forgotten meeting them, and met them again.

> When I landed, it was not on earth but on pure pain; not localized in my feet, but throughout my body.

Already, within the time, I began to remember the time.
When he had come towards me, only a few steps, he
had seemed to stagger—I thought, perhaps, the toe of
his mirror-black boot had accidentally encountered the
edge of the carpet (there were so many carpets and so
many edges).

When his eyes failed to focus upon me, for a moment, I
had believed it was because they were seeking out
vaster visions away in the East.

I would not have been at all insulted had the Führer
said, "Excuse me, Lieutenant, I have just had a thought
concerning China," and turned away from me—in fact,
I would have been ecstatic; perhaps I had been present
at one of those moments of great decision for which
the Führer had always been so famed—his instinct for
the absolutely right histrionic gesture.

Rage—rage like the milkless infant; and so the many
mothers try to feed him.

In his presence, one did certain things because those
were the things one did in his presence: it wasn't so
much worship as etiquette.

He was everything I needed to defeat, and I needed to
do so by showing absolute loyalty—and by believing
myself to be absolutely loyal.

I keep going back and back to the same memory, and
each time it finds a different way of being the same.

Hitler, in the flesh, makes one feel as if one's actions
might be significant—most of all when those actions are

in obedience to his will and are the obedient carrying
out of his orders.

I thought of the pipe out of the ornamental lake.

> When I land, it is clear straight away that it is bad—it is
> very, very bad.

Someone touched my arm again.

"It is time to leave," they said.

"You must leave, now," they said.

It felt wrong to turn my back on History, but History
had dismissed me—the World-Spirit had no more use
for such a trivial being.

> Upon my first capture behind enemy lines, I had been
> tortured. The Nazis had been experts in all methods.
> But nothing they had done to me, over those months,
> had been as totally excruciating as this.

They took me directly from the Führer to the plane.

For of course, I wished to cling.

> It was as if all of me had been struck at once, inside and
> out—I am not exaggerating; I never exaggerate.

Jens and Jurgen were with me, right up until the last
moment.

Jens and Jurgen dropped me out of the bomb doors of
the plane.

(I thought there was an animal nearby, making an awful moaning sound, then I realized the animal was I.)

I can't breathe for moments after, even as the agony fades away—or rather begins to localize itself in my left leg.

I had met the Führer and I hadn't killed the Führer.

I knew that I had done something pretty damn serious to the leg—a sprain or a fracture, it didn't really matter which: if I wasn't able to move fast enough to make certain rendezvous points, the mission was essentially buggered.

Remember: ignorance.

And the Führer wanted me to kill Churchill for him.

It hurts—it hurts so much that I don't know—I don't know what to do—I don't know how to be—how to feel this much pain and yet still be in any way at all.

A gentleman should greet agony very much as if he were greeting his old Latin master.

With my kiboshed leg out of action, I crawled away from the landing site as fast as I could. What an upcock that had been.

Once I was far enough away from the parachute— although I could still see it billowing like a vast creature from an evil dimension—I hid myself away in a copse.

And I so very much wanted to kill my grandfather.

A copse—an English copse!—are there such things any-where else in the world?

In the scrotty tangle of neglected, ungamekept England—this is where my boyhood had taken place, this is where I most truly belong.

Truth be told, I felt more at home in the place at this moment—despite my agony—than at any time before or since.

Yes, my desire has been granted: I am back home, back in the thick of the thicket (just the ticket), just as I had long wished, yearned for.

The ankle begins to swell—I can feel it pressing against the insides of my boot.

I gave myself a few moments to take the old place in—grabbed a fistful of dirty, dry August dirt, and just held it up to my nose and mouth. I wanted to eat it. I did so want to eat it.

Oh, I had been away so long—not perhaps in my lifetime, but out of the years I could consciously remember.

I am twenty-four, and have been a prisoner of war for a fifth of that.

I was twenty-four, and I had come home.

And I want to kill my grandfather.

Another gush of pain flooded through me; the boot was beginning to feel unbearably tight around the swelling ankle.

I stick my tongue out and let it rest on the dusty top of the earth. Why isn't the earth edible? Why is it, I think, that only worms and little boys can consume soil?

Once up a time, before the war, someone travelling through deepest China had brought me back some tea that seemed to consist entirely of pieces of black bark. It was, they informed me, over twenty-five years old, and pretty close to the best of its sort. When I brewed up, without milk, it was my boyhood come back again—even though the soil it had come from could hardly have been more remote had it been the sands of Alice Springs. The thought of that tea makes me wish I could have boiled up a billy can, thrown in some choice pieces of what I found around me, and drunk the whole Darkenings off in one draught.

Undergrowth was where I grew up, on my own—I would crawl into the thickest thicket I could find, finding a way beneath the lowliest branches; then, safe within a circle of my own imagining, I would do with myself exactly as I wished. Many were the tests of strength and courage I forced myself to endure.

Of course, in the end, I developed a special place—a camp—where I would keep and bury things, ready for me to return to them.

If something—a toy soldier—spent time under-the-ground, overnight, its specialness increased. The process of gaining specialness was mysterious, but somehow the abandonment and retrieval taught a plastic soldier to be tougher in battle.

Perhaps this present damage was to increase my specialness.

I can see where I learnt that lesson, and it was not at my grandfather's knee; my grandfather's knee was up in town, on business that involved much kneeling, I now believed. (Would you call it business, though?)

My heart had slowed to inaudibility, and my ears could hear across the surface of my rough breathing— between the hillocks.

Soon I realize I have begun listening because there is something to hear: a smooth-engined car coming along a country lane.

At least the car was just one, on its own—though any car could contain four or five armed men. The Home Guard.

I had only been down a few minutes; unless they had been up and dressed and gathered and drinking tea, the local boys couldn't have mustered themselves half so quickly.

The only explanation is that I have been betrayed, and they have been forewarned of my arrival. That, though, would still suggest the presence of more than one car.

If they'd known a spy was there for the taking, the whole village would have been out, supervised by the staff of The House Beautiful, supervised by the Gamekeeper.

If they'd known the spy was myself, it would have become a festival, a fête, audible even before I'd landed.

The single car changed gear.

I could see the fat headlights white down below Crackback Ridge—off in the direction of Midford.

The car—the car—is coming towards me, but that involves a long traverse from left to right, West to East.

There is something truly sublime about headlights down a country lane.

The long yellow beam-cones lit up the hedgerows to either side of the Tarmacadam.

When the car passes beneath a tree, it seems to become the centre of a slow explosion; wink.

I could not make out the model or make of the car; it did not have blue lights on the top. I thought it was probably a tourer of some sort, a saloon. Perhaps a Healey or a Rover. Just the kind of car the local Dad's Army would use. Just the sort of thing the Gamekeeper would use—he was, I knew, running the whole shebang around these parts. Before the war, he had been the proud, not to say arrogant, owner of an Austin 11, and he wasn't likely to have had the chance to trade it in after the outbreak of hostilities.

At a ninety-degree turn in the road, the lights for an instant flashed in my direction.

Night sight of white light across the hedgerow, and where am I now in the all-woebegone? And something here about devastating fear—I was devastated by fear, something like that.

Irrationally, buried as I was deep in the undergrowth, I feared they would be able to spot me.

In the headlights, I was able to catch sight of my ankle, bulging over the top of my left boot.

The boots weren't shiny, soldierly, but the kind of flap-bottomed indecency you would expect of a tramp. And they were of English manufacture, originally. The SS wouldn't tell me how on earth they'd come by them.

The car went past a field of cows; I saw their spotty sides projected in long Autumn shadows across the grass. This image stayed with me a long while before time restarted again, and the car passed out of sight.

But not out of hearing; it was the only loudness amidst the quiet.

With two pointing fingers, I traced it—eyes closed—up the Midford Road.

With each passing moment the car draws nearer.

Listening to the engine, however, it sounds merely driven rather than really driven. One feels the driver is at his ease. And now they bottom out from second to first—a little too late—at the brow of the hill. I even guess they might have been imbibing.

At its closest point, the engine gave a growl, a hiccough, then a bang—this damn near loosed my bowels, so like was it to the firing squads that had accompanied my sleepless frozen mornings in the camp.

But the car passes—the car does finally pass—down the more gradual side of the hill, past the village sign and into Amplewick proper; and the sound of it changes as it goes between two rows of brick cottages.

I thought, if I followed it closely enough, I might be able to tell at which house it stopped. And I was right: at the crossroads it paused, then it pulled away—down Unstable Street, towards Flathill. After reaching the bottom of the next dip, it turned off, probably to the left, and parked very soon.

I let it go; it was no possible threat to me now.

Without being aware of it, I had taken a thick stick and placed it in my mouth, as if I were a salivating dog—as if, had they come upon me with torches, a stick like this might have made them mistake me for one of the pack hounds.

The night has its quiet, far from silence, returned to it once more (the combustion engine is now too far away to disturb; in fact, it consoles).

The bite marks in the stick are an error, a giveaway: I will have to carry it with me, until I can burn it.

One knew one should move immediately, but with the threat of the car gone one took a few more preparatory deep breaths. Pain; imminent.

All right, if it has to be done it has to be done. But then I am entirely stopped, even before I have half-lifted myself to my feet—an unbelievable vision of unlikelihood is forming itself almost directly over my head.

Christ! The parachute canopy was detaching itself from the oak tree, quite as if it had truly become a live jelly-fish and had decided—Can jellyfish be said to make or take decisions?—to arise and go.

An updraught of very constant air could be the only rational explanation, ascending the hill and pushing the silk equally at every point. But there were no tree-waves around me, no above-rustling.

The night had returned to a stillness approaching airlessness.

Yet there the canopy is, lifting, the strings now no longer gathered around the central me but diffusing to the edges—making the apparition even more jellyfish-like.

Up it went, up until it had cleared the tree entirely. My heart beat maybe once or twice this whole minute, and I swear I didn't breathe. I felt like the canopy was turning all of a sudden into a vast black ghost, and then whooshing off to find some poor soul to spook. Then, in a moment, the whole mushroom-top collapsed and, at the same time, leapt upwards and away. As it rose, ripples shimmered all through it, quite as if it were pulsingly alive or spectrally possessed.

The thing must be possessed—from a jellyfish (remem-bered now as benign) it had transformed into a sea-lion or a dolphin, for it shimmered away through the air, not out across the High Field but towards the deepest depths of The Darkenings.

Never have I seen anything so uncanny; all I can hope is that this freak wind (which I didn't feel) will do as it seems to have done, and stow my advertisement somewhere less conspicuous.

The Darkenings had always been for me a place of fear but also of respite, safety. As long as I was only there during the hours of daylight, I felt quite at home—though the prickle-sensation of being-watched never quite went away.

As a boy of eleven, I had come to believe many things of The Darkenings—that it was quite thrillingly haunted by thrown-away dolls, by The Smelly People, by wood-spirits, and that a witch of great age and ugliness resided towards the darkest midpoint, in a standard-issue witch's hut.

Later still, as I grew and was allowed into adult tales, my beliefs were joined by rumours of bizarre rites practised here by heathen tribes in the time before history. Darkness of blood.

These village rumours had it that The Darkenings was so called for very good reason. One local historian even had it that The Darkenings was a corruption of the even more suggestive The Hearkenings.

If you slept here, we used to tell one another at school—if you were brave enough to stay here overnight—the trees would begin to whisper to you all of the things that they had witnessed, across the centuries. At least four murders had happened here. The older rumours of ritual sacrifice had never died in the mouths of the villagers.

Was I to be terrified again by the spooky-creaky place, as I had been as a boy? It seemed so—it very much seemed so.

I had come to believe many things of The Darkenings—

That I had tried to find the said witch, and had found a cottage some might have called a hut; certainly in comparison to The House Beautiful, it could even have been described as a *hovel*.

That I was scared away from the small house with the slate roof by a thing that, I still to this day believe, flew out of the door and towards my head with eyes, teeth, claws and wings in no particular order.

These were the things that I remembered—although I suspected that during the eternal twilight of my boyhood, there had been superstitiously many many more—flitting in and around the trees—some involving being unable to breathe, some involving rat battalions, some involving slime and death, and some involving death quite unadorned.

The black canopy had moved off towards the centre of the wood, and that seemed the safest place for me, too—given the circumstances. If the parachute was found, they would call the hounds—the pack from The House Beautiful. I would still know some of them— Clement, Elder, Eeler, Jangle, Gordon, Ethelred, Nash and Wishful—and I was sure they would remember me, once they had my scent beneath their noses. Eagerly would they pursue.

In my imagination I can already hear them breaking into cry, lolloping off in pursuit of me, giving tongue as they came.

Good would be to put some stretch of water between myself and them—confuse and delay. Even better, I needed to hitch a ride high up on a very smelly and fast-moving machine for a few miles. But nothing of that suitable sort would be around in the silence of this night—and even if it were, it would be too dangerous for me to avail myself of it. What mere farmer had driving-business at two o'clock in the morning? With my damaged foot, I could never have caught him up, not unless he slowed almost as if he knew he was collecting me.

During the time I'd been delaying, my ankle had swollen as much as it was going to. Keeping my boot on was becoming the worst agony I had ever known—including torture by the Gestapo in a provincial Bavarian town where they rarely got the chance to torture anyone. But I knew that if I took the boot off—cut the laces—I would never be able to get it back on.

A dog started barking somewhere, now—a domestic dog, a pug or a poodle. Sounds travelled deceptively on a windless night like this—there was water nearby, the ornamental lake. If the dog were beyond that, it could be miles away.

I stood up, cried out, stuck my knuckles into my mouth and bit. First, I needed a stick to support me as I hobbled—a crutch of some sort, shoulder high with a V at the top. V for Victory. In the dark, such a prodigious item would be almost impossible to find. I had a torch but, in the circumstances, could hardly risk it.

Better would be the crutches of a veteran—they would be more efficient and less conspicuous. I would have to work towards stealing them. Such thoughts were for the future—if I had a future.

I collapsed—the pain was too great.

The conditions in our camp were nowhere near as bad as those in Other Camps.

Let me describe my pain. But that is not possible. You are not capable of remembering. We none of us are. Do you think I am interested in reading descriptions of pain? The only time we have any curiosity about pain is when it is being inflicted upon us or we are inflicting it upon others. In the former case it is ravishing; in the latter, glamorous. Let me recreate my pain, as best I can. Far better. If only I could. If only . . .

No, it's no use. The game is most definitely up. I pull the cyanide collar towards my mouth, then realize I might as well wait. In such pain, I am unlikely to fall asleep. I can as well kill myself when my enemies are ten feet away and approaching as when I am, as far as I know, merely injured, at bay and unmenaced.

I could watch the sun come up one last time, that was my thought.

The topmost branches moved, wavered once, as if the parachute were returning, back from its episode of haunting. I had watched gliders landing on the airfield in Germany—they were practising for behind-the-lines missions just as I had been. The passing whoosh of air was not unlike theirs, although a deal more fluttery.

It was at this point that The Darkenings began to assume its old character for me, the one it had taken when I was a boy: eyes were staring at me. Disembodied eyes. Eyes that had just rolled up, by themselves, in pairs. I was sure I could see them, looking towards me out of the darkness.

The clouds had knitted themselves together in front of the minimal moon. This was as black and impenetrable a night as any I had ever known. It was my safety; it was my threat. No-one could possibly sneak up upon me, yet I was unable to move.

I was comforting myself with the thought of a few more hours' consciousness before obliteration when I thought I heard my old nanny's voice, singing me a lullaby, telling me—in-between lines—that all would be all right and my head would be clear if I just went to sleep. The song was so comforting, I almost believed Nanny Taylor had found me out there in the dark and cold.

It was cold.

I knew not what kind of hallucination it might be.

In the camp: my frigid form, witness.

I could see my nanny's singing face. Lines were coming out of her mouth, red lines, not blood, straight red lines like her wool being pulled tight.

Had I injured myself in some place I didn't know, and was beginning hallucinations heralding death?

Was I bleeding out?

Is this how it ends?

They took me to the camp after they caught me and
after they tortured me.

My last thought was to bury the knife, a prisoner's trick.

I couldn't see anything, but I could feel—and I knew this
tree; I knew it had humpy roots.

Different flavours of indifference.

There is a hold here that seems made for the purpose.

I put the knife in a hole in the tree—down under the
roots.

In the silver barracks several things took place; harmonics.

One feels greatly privileged to have been allowed to suffer as one has.

I should take the cyanide, but I am being sung to sleep
and I want to sleep, and it's so nice to hear female
singing—warm, like the radiogram.

It has been, I think, at least three years since there was
no dirt beneath my fingernails.

The Heer at this time still maintained a tradition of pretending to observe its traditions; spook.

If I took the cyanide, I would not really sleep; if I sleep, I
may never have to take the cyanide.

Have you ever looked really closely at the grain in a
piece of wood? I mean really closely? I mean for three
days?

I shaved in a spoon, on weekdays concave, on weekends
convex; the mirror had gone to be fashioned into knives.

Smell of the left hand holding the lower edge of the
photograph of Betty Grable; Life.

When violence happens, our first sliver of time-reaction
is always joy in shocking pink.

> As if from outside, I watch my eyes closing; as if my
> face were a face very close to my face

As if from outside, I watch my eyes closing; as if my
face were a face very close to my face.

Gift: That of which we were no longer capable:
distancing.

A man eating another man who was not quite dead and
therefore fresh meat but moaning. I only imagined that.

Overboiled cabbage—if we were lucky, overboiled
cabbage; dose.

A gentleman should never pass comment on his
latest meal, no more than he would upon his latest
evacuation.

Human desire, how mortifying a spectacle; bone-chase.

I have been sold by one man to another for a half dozen cigarettes, although—in the event—I was used by neither of them.

What you can imagine of torture is always happening somewhere on the surface of earth—and if, by some chance, you are the very first to imagine it, it will start happening somewhere a few minutes later (after the torturers return, refreshed, from their break). This is how the world innovates.

Bruise-child: Raids on resources that no longer exist, if only to maintain morale.

Shuffle. When men smelled of mildew and mildew smelled of trust. Shuffle.

Singing singing—that was the last of this black particular night I was to know.

"If you try to escape, you will be shot."

Seeing damage being done yet refraining from intervening; war-chords.

The things I might have done with a knife, if it hadn't been confiscated; the ways I might have expressed my inner self.

Labour: Our fingernails do not need cutting or biting.

The green grass in green water in a jamjar with a lid embossed with narrow black and white stripes; vertical; gift.

Heartleft: The things which fall down from below us;
the things which erupt from nowhere but the sky; the
things that plunge directly through our backs, arriving
in a second from a thousand miles away.

I remember women less frequently than I remember
men, but I remember them more vividly. Not specific
women: the idea of specific women.

The cuntish obscenity of that sunset over ice; diseased
whores lifting their skirts to advertise themselves to
passing battalions.

Smell of a photograph of the aroused pudenda of
Marilyn Monroe, thing.

Smell of the engine oil beneath the fingernails of a left
hand holding a trembling photograph of Betty Grable;
available.

We like to imagine what an actress in Hollywood smells
like, on the days she has to work beneath hot lights.

I am thinking of food; mist.

Smell of a freshly opened packet of a well-known brand
of breakfast cereal; cornflakes.

My fingers wanted to write, but my hands hadn't been
allowed the materials. We were denied paper and pen.
What if I had managed to draw a map of the camp?
What if we had begun to forge papers, permits,
passports?

How we return always to our tongues, burrow.

The boundary between conformity and identity is always sweetly marked by barbed wire.

One remembers men so agonized they began to miaow.

You will not try to escape and so you will not be shot. You try to be a model prisoner, as they say. It must have worked. (Scale model prisoner.)

I tried to give him some of my rations, but he wouldn't accept—so I began to slip extra crumbs onto his plate when he wasn't looking. I also imagined this.

I wish there was a tabby cat to stroke.

When it's too exhausted to function in any other way, the military body will still obey the order to march. Shuffle.

Good omens multiply in bad times.

I continue to endure loneliness, despite marching.

The blossoming of the realization that one's mouth is in extremely close proximity to shit.

Boots have very little grandeur to those whose life does not depend on them. There are, as far as I am aware, no great poems about boots.

When I could I spoke, when I couldn't I grunt-sang.

At a certain point during my youth, what I wore was far more important to me than what I thought; then, as I aged and became more mature, as I suffered, I found that I had entirely ceased caring about what I thought, paying no mind to anything beyond the success of that day's outfit. This might be my autobiography, too.

My time in the camp removed these beauteous concerns; when one is starving, one is not unaware of one's growing beauty but too enervated to do anything with it.

XYZ: I was fast getting to the weight—lack of weight— where Auschwitz coincides with *Vogue*.

My time in the camp removed the vanity of my person as thoroughly as it did the enamel of my teeth.

Beauty is youth welcoming new forms of discipline; lenient.

An aphorism is a way for us to imagine we agree with that which is purely objectionable, because it is the thought—lace-froth—of another.

Men standing in lines are different to men not standing in lines.

See this sentence—a young man vomits his bowels. I mean, see what happens in this sentence.

Men standing in lines are made of a softer hardness than men not standing in lines.

Your loss becomes your gift.

Rooks are constructed from black bile.

Thin finds ways to become thinner; teeth can lose weight.

I could recall almost nothing of life immediately before Germany. The House Beautiful was in my head, and the ways around it—public galleries to secret passages. I could also recall the location of certain trees in The Darkenings. Beyond that, it was a bland potage of unspecific boredoms and anxieties. I felt certain something had come between me and my identifying-signifying memories—something to do with horror of falling. However, during this everlasting month, I did not have time to pre-occupy myself with anything beyond mere survival. The check is in the past.

A note for the future I once made: "Accumulate regrets, or you'll regret it."

You will know when you have said too much when you look around and see that the men listening with the greatest pleasure are your greatest enemies.

I became extremely negative and then I became an object of interest; I must have talked too much, about the wrong things.

"Please, follow me," the guard said, when no-one was within hearing. And when I heard "Please" in English, I knew I was about to be invited to be a traitor.

You have a house. You have a grandfather. You have a knife.

There are details which I do not believe to be credibly real, details to do with how he held and smoked and crushed his cigarette.

Your house is a famous house. Your grandfather is an influential man. Your knife is a sharp knife.

"You should be happy," they said. "We have something special for you."

A man with silver swastikas on his collars was politely inviting one to kill one's grandfather—one could hardly say no, now could one?

To return to England, I would betray anything I had not betrayed in order to leave. Yet I felt strongly that I should do what they asked me to do.

I left the camp at night; everyone would be told that I had tried to escape; I would be the talk of breakfast and perhaps lunch—my name garlanded with barbed wire.

One hates being taken out of one's box almost as much as one hates one's box.

From the helmets of the guards sprouted bouquets of breath, downwards.

One hates leaving one's prison almost as much as one hates one's prison.

The engine of the car was so big that it warmed one, even though one was sitting in the back seat.

I went from being a prisoner to being a soldier, without noticing.

This is my car journey. I should enjoy it, but I sleep solid until we jerk to a cold stop.

German dawns—is the sun trying to tell the Fatherland something? An off egg cracked onto a placenta.

The only difference between soldiers and prisoners is that soldiers get to see their priest running.

Jens and Jurgen threw me out of an aeroplane, repeatedly, for a week. I should say that by the end we almost became friends.

Soldiers are prisoners with horizons; Prisoners are soldiers without ammunition.

It is hard to believe that Jens and Jurgen had not been cut out of a poster, using a good razor. In turbulence, their epaulettes would bruise my eyebrows. Occasionally, one of them would pick me up and pass me to the other, as if I were a boy. They glowed like apples.

"You have with Winston Churchill met?" Jurgen asked.

> He didn't know where he was and he didn't know who he was but he knew at least that the he who didn't know who he was was a he; seemingly.

"You have Winston Churchill before once met?" Jens asked.

A prisoner does not believe he is a soldier; the opposite is not true.

The man who packs your parachute for you is your best friend, whether you hate him or not.

Despite myself, despite trying not to, I think forwards to catching a clear sight of The House Beautiful as I fall from the sky. Not The Darkenings, though—I know that one never gets a clear sight of The Darkenings.

Jens taught me in English and allowed me to count in English, but if I got above a certain number, he punished me in German.

I see myself, despite myself, running until I am safe and then I am bending down and kissing the ground; the ground seems to kiss me back.

My knife was returned; the knife with which I arrived in Germany; it had a brown-paper tag on it, with a name and a date and three different numbers. Such a bureaucracy should surely have won this war.

Death is an inhuman facility.

All my dreams, without exception, are of falling, without end; puff.

> Opening his eyes, he found that his eyes weren't opening —that his eyes wouldn't/couldn't open; not even the slightest little bit.

These Germans are certainly marvellous creatures—if one could only stop them eating so many potatoes!

That's what this whole damned war is all about, potatoes.

"Lebensraum" is German for "potato patch".

"Potato-stealer" is German for "Jew".

Down by his sides, his hands were too weak—because too exhausted—to make the long aching journey to the face.

I imagine the taxi, take-off, climb, cruise at altitude as if I had experienced them as a boy; the man I have become had no access to their pleasure. It was a relief not to be touching Germany; it was almost a joy to be saying farewell to Jens and Jurgen. The boy would have looked out of the window and appreciated what he saw. The boy would have been excited about his black silk parachute. The man thinks he is aware of what going home means.

I can now distinguish the different smells of three different kinds of engine oil.

> He knew he was no longer outside, because the sounds were different. He knew it was no longer night, because the light was different. His eyes feel prickly, though perhaps it is too early to introduce this.

That would be Berlin, then. It smells of burnt potato.

The sea from on high looks more like a million small mountains than, by rights, it should.

> He lies not upon leaves but upon a bed of softness, which involves—he feels—sheets and probably blankets; his hand touches the side of his hip and finds it to be naked.

> They aren't military blankets, he knows this; they are lighter, less tightly woven, less oily.

I am not a bluebird; the thought makes me laugh.
Fields. Really near to it.

"He" becomes me and I perceive light, I feel objects;
everything, in short, is in some kind of order.

The thought: I have woken in England without pain.

"You should more happy," they once said. "You will the
Führer soon meet."

The first sound I manage to make is not a word, although
I intend it as a question.

I listened for the reply, and thought I heard breathing of
an animal that did not want to be heard.

The voice I expected to hear was the voice of my mother
being told not to speak by the voice of my grandfather.

"Hello?" was the word beneath the next sound that my
throat made.

"You must smile," they said. "You will the Führer soon
meet."

I thought I knew the difference between the creak of a
tree in the wind and the creak of a chair when weight
shifts.

I make some other sounds, one after another, to see if I
can get a sense of the place I am in. They do not echo,
they are not unduly muffled-dulled. Not a cathedral and
not a cupboard—but I knew that. Somewhere domestic.

I try to see through my eyelids; I concentrate on my face, which is visited by only the slightest of breezes; I inhale, and smell blankets.

What I imagine to be a minute passes. The right half of my vision was redder than the left half; and, when yellow, yellower; and, when near-white, whiter.

Also, the air comes slightly more keenly to my right cheek. I feel or think I feel the convection of air, tendril-like, towards a cold vertical surface. I get that sensation of being close to a cold pane of glass which sucks heat towards it before the sun warms it through.

The camp had made me a connoisseur of blankets: a bad or wet one and hypothermia and death; a superb one might have you murdered in your sleep.

This place was not a place in which I would spend frozen nights; some tearful gratitude for this. Oh, Christ, whatever else, at least I am not in Poland!

Our blankets came, we knew, from the disinherited Jews who travelled. Some of the blankets arrived smelling of cats or perfume or urine.

If I were to move, I would find more out; I must there-fore move. Knowledge is a good. It seems I still have both elbows.

What do I remember? There was a long journey followed by a short rest followed by a long journey followed by the word follow.

My left foot touches my right foot, touches fabric on my right foot, touches a bandage or a poultice.

Hello, pain. Hello again.

I did, I admit, scream; and a female voice, young and low but crackly, close but not near, said, "Hush you there now."

When I could, I spoke; I asked question after question: "Where am I?"—"Where am I?"—"Who are you?"— "Where are my clothes?"— "Was it you who bandaged my ankle?"—"What are you going to do with me?"— "Am I a prisoner?"—"Are you the witch that lives here?"—"Are you still there?"—"Are you still here?"— But, after these first four words, she did not speak to me; she did not even allow her breathing to become expressive—no yawns, no supple sighs; the creak of a nearby tree.

Then there is movement, fast movement towards me— so I think—and I fall asleep.

The singing I heard before was not my nanny singing; it was the sound of having no choice but to fall asleep.

Blank gap.

When I re-awoke, I thought I was back dangling in the tree again. It was a nightmare of hanging-falling-hanging-falling that had awoken me, with anguish.

I suppose I treat the first time I wake as a dream slipping across to a nightmare: softness, blindness, blankets. The second time, I make the attempt to gain definitive answers from it.

No watch upon my wrist; no clock in the place—at least, no ticking: in fact, no rhythmic sound whatsoever.

With-wing-listening, like any moth.

Simply, "Hello there?"

I listened: there was a general twitter of birds, of tits over to my right—perhaps through an open window?—all in a bush or tree, from which I tried to eke out the great, the blue, the willow—and for a few moments, despite their chivvying, I thought I had; but then an unusually avant-garde robin redbreast arrived, breaking up the stability of the aural landscape.

These would be the natural sounds of The Darkenings, during daylight hours.

Beyond the close birds are other birds; wood-pigeons, for example; more intermittent. You do do, you do. You do do, you do.

In the distance I could hear the hounds of the pack in their kennels—and I believed I could make out individual voices—or at least family resemblances; bitch and pup.

In the furthest distance, I could hear cows bellowing, so I knew I was within a shortish walk of the farm belonging to the house.

It was sweet to be back close to such familiarities, even in anguish.

I have awoken in England with pain.

"Hello?" I asked but the crackly woman didn't reply, and I didn't hear her breathing however hard I strained—and the straining made it hard to hear, it brought the blood-rush alive in my head, so I gave up.

When we have nothing else, breathing becomes a great pleasure.

My ankle is painful enough to keep me awake, this time, if I put left foot on top of right. It has been dressed with rough bandages, carefully.

I feel genuine panic over having lost my eyesight, which last time I woke seemed like a typical nightmare. (What might the witch choose to do to me? But then, wouldn't she have done it already? Perhaps she had.)

When I tried to move my hands, they responded as if I were wearing a suit of armour. The hands seemed to want to move and to be capable of moving, the medium of restriction was outside them.

The image of myself, laid out, the family tomb, a stone knight clutching his sword beneath gauntlets.

One could not be sure one was hearing what one was hearing. Threaded through the birdsong; unthreading from the blankets.

It is not my nanny; she is not singing.

When I woke up for a third time, I managed to persuade one of my stone hands to drag itself to my eyes— which felt strange. They didn't hurt, but the eyelashes seemed particularly prickly. I brought up my other hand, energized by panic, and ran fingertips along from side to side, eyelid and eyelid. They felt what they felt: stitches; Bang.

Like the false step when running across bracken; the rabbit hole, the collapsing grey sand.

Stitches on the bottom of each eyelid and stitches on the soft skin of my face beneath the lower lid. Someone—this young woman who had said "Hush you there now"—someone has sewn my eyes shut.

Like the bottom jaw punching the top jaw with a judder; the teeth immediately aching, not broken; the top of the head feeling as if it has been loosened by the bash of the brain.

A gentleman should behave no differently in a prison than in a palace—to be affected by place shows lack of character.

I tried to sit up but my stomach muscles felt cramped; they wouldn't bend for me.

Since finding the stitches, I had been screeching or screaming or wailing—from inside the sound, it was hard to tell. My jaw muscles felt stretched/exercised, so screaming was the more likely.

"Get them off!" was the sentence which emerged when I made out my own sense. "Get them out of me!"

For a while now I cannot hear for my own noise.

"Quiet," said the woman. "Be quiet." Her voice was standing on the other side of the room or whatever-space—out of my reach. She does not sound amused, but she does sound sexual.

I would have tried to move, to walk, but I was too weak to try to move, to rise.

My next sentence involves a threat and draws forth a laugh. "As if you ever could," the woman says, and sounds almost weary.

How soon needling turns to wheedling.

The fear she would do something to me in my helpless state.

"I need to see," I said. "Please. I will die if I can't see. You don't understand."

"No," she replied. "Not yet. Not till I know I can trust you. And that'll be a while yet."

The older one gets, the more one realizes how many moments there are when one shouldn't speak.

But I told her that she couldn't just go round sewing men's eyes shut when they were asleep—to which she replied, "They're fighting a war, aren't they? You might be a German spy."

"You know who I am," I say, and I tell her my name.

She is silent with her mouth, although I could hear her hands doing things. Their movements were skittery-agitated, as if they were picking small stones up and putting them down, or rolling tiny ivory poker dice, or perhaps I was wrong and it was just a rosary or worry beads or knitting.

"No," she said, after a few minutes of clicks, "Everybody knows that the son is dead."

The older one gets, the more one realizes how many moments there are when one absolutely shouldn't speak.

"I know who you are," I am saying. "I've seen you before. You are Olwyn. You are a witch. This is where you live, in the middle of The Darkenings."

And then I say, "My father lets you live here. If he didn't let you, they would clear you out. Everyone knows you're a witch. Only a witch would sew a man's eyes shut."

And the woman said, "Any woman would, if she could."

And so I say, "My father visits you, in the night."

"Oh," said the woman, "sooner or later they all visit me, in the night."

She does not speak any more, whatever I say, and as long as she is silent, I can imagine whatever I want about her.

Because I was blinded, she hadn't needed to introduce herself. Eat wood.

What she has said is thought-food for quite some time: If I had been captured, there would not be softness or women, and they would be trying to wake me, not lull me back to sleep.

What I think is that I must have woken these three times firstly in the morning, secondly the afternoon and lastly in the evening.

The morning had been white in the right-hand side of everything; the afternoon turns speckly golden; the evening greens.

The longer the day goes on, the more the most laborious birds take over the job of singing; wood-pigeons, for example. Do you.

We are all of us baked of different substances throughout the day. We start as fresh white bread and end as chocolate cake, but in-between we have passed through a digestive-biscuity phase.

During the evening my eyes descended through plum to purple to momentary velvet green and then flared to violet and peach as a candle was lit then fell away to areas of average red.

An inhead-discothèque; inappropriate morning; obvious anachronism.

I could feel the wall to my right, cool plaster with smooth paint on top.

There wasn't much else to feel—during the evening, that evening.

When I moved my left hand further up, I felt the surface become rougher—so this was Olywn's sleeping place,

and as she moved around, over the years, she had polished the whitewash with elbow grease.

Above the paint was a cold ledge and then, about as far
as I could reach, windowpanes.

Tap, tap with fingernails—that was glass.

Something touched me, a leaf; I explored the shape of
it.

I admire the ivy for not breaking the window to enter but
I admire the window more for opening to admit the ivy.

My left hand came back to my face feeling gritty,
smelling dusty—adhered to by spider's webs.

Back up again, my forefinger tinkles through another
web—each strand giving off a ping too high to hear but
not to sense. This is a fresh web, though; not one that
has caught dust.

> I am back there now. I do see patterns but they always
> seem to become other patterns just before I can recog-
> nize them. In this head-world, you can't be definite
> about anything.

There was another smoothed-off patch, even softer than
the elbow-one, right beside my head. Here the wall
dented in, as if this were where the back of Olywn's
skull inveterately came to rest at day's end.

I pulled the blankets over my head and found I could
smell Olywn's womanhood.

60

She was savoury and sweet, like the air in a restaurant where cod and chips with salt and vinegar are being served on one table next to a table where they are already eating bread-and-butter pudding with vanilla custard.

This was not an old woman's smell.

> Head: What I want to say is there were strings which reached out to other strings in the attempt to become blobs of evaporatingness that condensed again as a rain-wash of plush ink, leaving trickle-traces after running down a sheet of uneven green glass containing bubbles that didn't simply rise over centuries but rotated in sets of circles.

The camp had stunk of piss, shit, vomit, mud, metal and smoke; the camp had stunk—that is to say—of men's mechanized fears.

Adolf Hitler had the fragrance of ginger biscuits, Coca-Cola, blood and Christmas.

> What I want to say is that a red grid attacked by acid green was dissolved until only spindles were left, each unconnected with the other, which dwindled until they were pinpricks which bled, and again but unevenly there was red to flood and flow towards a centre which clearly became a collecting bowl for (for this was blood) coagu-lation and afterwards clotting, smearing, here and there.

As the night came on, I thought I heard the songs of birds native to Germany; birds I was sure I hadn't heard whilst there—if I had been there.

As I began to fall asleep, I thought I heard—sound of
my childhood—the London train. As I began to fall
asleep, I thought I heard—sound of war—a Lancaster
bomber

> What I want to say is the flare in the camera's lens is
> turned to spun sugar that shatters at a touch when
> attacked by marshmallow dots of pink coming out of
> nowhere, all at once, spangle-made, dozens of them
> against a background of indigo silk which the bright
> light begins immediately to cause to fade through puce,
> ultramarine and piss-yellow as the pink dots turn to
> puffs of stringy smoke that get lost among one another
> again and again until a tumbling starts which makes me
> nauseous the closer it comes to being a proper vortex in
> my head, of my head—whirling like time-lapse stars or
> soapy water down the bath hole or the whole world
> when you've twirled and twirled yourself to collapsing
> on the top of a high hill or the first time you are really
> drunk and the roomspin kicks in; and there is nothing to
> stop it, unless I look right and stare towards the bright-
> est light source I can, and will that to seem a fixed point.
>
> But it isn't, the point, is always woozy, although strong
> enough a one-presence to churn up the anti-clockwise
> and bring it to the comfort of the chaotic. Until the eye-
> patterns begin once again to reform.

Even if my eyes had not been sewn shut, I doubt if I
could have seen anything.

> Sometimes it is wallpapers I am sure I have seen in some
> Victorian house; sometimes it is television watched via
> the projection on the ceiling of an upstairs room you
> are waiting outside the house of; sometimes it is coal

falling into the coalhole until the day comes through but only in chinks; sometimes it is the surface of the sea seen upwards, through seaweed.

There are granular constellations of red-orange-pink floating high above a background whose colour I still can't decide upon—perhaps a field of poppies seen through a glass of Ribena or very dark polaroid glasses, or a pint of my blood admixed with two tablespoons of black ink. Or is it just a palimpsest of signatures practising themselves?

I knew I would fall again into dreams of falling.

When I cover my eyes with the crook of my arm, the left eye going into my upper arm, the right into my forearm, so they are into the corner of a triangle missing on one side, the colours are all deeper and modulate, oranges becoming reds, reds becoming purples, greens becoming aubergines. They super-add blue rather than black. Browns are extremely rare, although, by controlling how much light hits me, I have done the rainbow spectrum in roygbiv order.

At the bottom is a bulge, a rounded-off hillock, of cheeks.

When I began to sculpt with light, I found I could use my brows to create diagonals, triangular shadows.

With some effort, my held-up fingers made clear stripes of violet which interrupted the pink.

One knew it was the middle of the night because one knew one had already begun to fall back asleep again.

I could smell and feel the bobbly sheets and webby blankets—the wool balling up and forming fibres across the surface, the cotton going granular.

In fact, as I—connoisseur—discovered throughout that next day's exploration, there were many of Olwyn's blankets upon me.

Lord, there are so many blankets on top of me that I feel like a shallow beach, with wave after wave coming in.

Having little else to do, apart from make eye-patterns and breathe the air and listen to birdsong, I explored the length of each blanket-edge with my fingertips. These were old coverings, with a great deal of character. I breathe differently to how I remember—more like a straightforward man; less cowardly. The parachute jump may have changed something. Birdsong is almost irritatingly beautiful.

After I had spent some serious time exploring my bedding, I changed the image of waves—quite consciously—for that of an organist with multiple keyboards rising in front of him. (Waves move, keyboards don't—the image was more accurate.) One of the higher keyboards (further-off blankets) had tassels which would do as stops. I even, down the bottom, had two layers near my feet which I could imagine as pedals.

I feel how lucky I am compared to some flameball pilot, stuck with starchy hospital bedclothes drumtight each afternoon.

These blankets have frayings, repairs in different threads and wools, patches, square and star-shaped patches.

One particular blanket—my chief delight—was a patch-work of differently knitted squares: different wools, different stitch patterns.

I do not entirely forget my knife.

The Darkenings were far, far above me; far too far.

Today, the birds in their songs seem repeatedly to be trying to pierce something. If it-the-thing isn't made of wood then it is probably made of bird.

From where I lay, altogether in the altogether, I could hear through the window the whole of it and the unity of it.

A twittering so dense it becomes substance; all it would take is a kiln-firing of these ear-haloes and one would have two china bowls.

As long as I made no effort to force reality into thought-forms, everything was clarity itself.

Look, the decision-monster, riding through its own crimson!

The birds were singing because the birds were singing because birds sing and birds listen and birds are just birds except when they are songs that other birds sing for other birds to listen to and so be turned into songs.

At first I think an earthquake is shimmering the land.

Through the open doorway, I thought I could hear the deep, rumbling throb of the engines of a—was it?—

Lancaster bomber. Quite far off: they weren't shaking anything on the shelves. The thing must have been forced to land for repairs, behind enemy lines, then taken off and made a low-altitude dash back across the Channel. The engines sounded a bit bloody ropey, extremely churny, as if they were constantly cutting out and starting up again. They purred for a few minutes, suggesting that the bomber was circling, awaiting permission to land. I knew there was an airbase quite close by, but I didn't understand why they weren't getting the crate out of the sky as soon as possible. Quite soon, I was to find out what had really been going on.

When did this occur? Day two or day four? Olwyn gives me tea, which tastes too bitter to be tea. It threatens to send me to sleep.

The birdsong and the wool began to relate to one another in strange rhythms.

At times I felt that my wool-organ was playing/controlling the tweets and chirrups and twitters and chirps outside.

At other times I felt the heads of each individual bird popping out of the holes in the wool, to make a contribution of a few notes and then retreat, cuckoo-clock fashion.

If not an organ then a musical score, and the only reason it wasn't completely accurate for every noise I heard was that I was looking at the wrong point of it because my braille sight-reading wasn't up to much.

The wood-pigeon's is the love song of Sisyphus.

There is a hailstorm in my eyeballs—upwards, out-wards, at a forty-five-degree angle.

Flux, and even thinking for a second "It is staying the same!" immediately chucks a hundred stones, in an evenly-spaced grid, into the not-stagnant pond. The flat visual field splashes to a pattern of squared interference and cross-stitch as water frays to fabric-like-hessian, and what was always behind is set a-wobble like the faraway blackcurrant jelly I think it might be—with pips so clear I feel I could pick them out, one by one, before they sprout into tulips darned from swastikas and ectoplasm. Was this on day three or day five?

And then there were the imagined pictures. When I was a child, I saw the laughing red-faced devil first thing after lights out—perhaps his face was the simplified filament of the lightbulb, retinally retained; perhaps he existed. I saw him and he laughed at me, as he did again now.

These aren't after-images as there have been no fore-images—they bloom from the flowerbed of my lucidity. It took me some time to order what I sensed into inside-smells and outside-smells, created-smells and naturally-occurring-smells.

Quite soon, I was watching staticky multi-coloured television—flashing on advertisements and children's television programmes, anything that had gone in momentarily but never before had a chance to show that it had stayed.

What I caught in Olywn's house, first of all, wasn't merely a specific smell, of known-flowers or home-ness, but was itself utterly familiar: I am here and I know every part of here and I have known it as long as I have known anything.

Some scents—those of dried grasses and simples—I knew could very well be inside or outside.

When it was dark I smelled wet vegetation, damp earth, ivy, plaster, straw.

When it was hot I smelled haze, dry earth, pine needles, rhododendrons.

When it was evening I smelled oak burning, butter, the bottom of a copper cooking pot, Lapsang Souchong.

But some smells were mobile, flexible, protean—I would think that brewing tea was wet grass being heated was a horse's steaming urine was Olwyn's spit singing on a red iron.

A fox passed by, of that much I was certain. He was too vivid, as if he were a burning tyre filled with horsehair. This visit might, in turn, lead to a visit from the hunt—unless we had a day or two's rain; a familiar smell.

Every morning, Olwyn goes to fetch water from the well. The journey, back and forth, the drawing up—it all takes her about half an hour. If she doesn't do it, we will be thirsty. You have not mentioned the arrangement with food, drink.

I sometimes felt I was deliberately being tricked. That animals were being encouraged to come close to me and deposit their odours, in order to bamboozle. Had Olwyn invited the fox to saunter by? The badger to drop his faeces? The hare to waft a smidgeon of must my way? The deer to startle me with their rankness? The cows to splat, splat, splat, far away but many?

Lying abed I dealt with the senses discreetly, one by one—hue, heft, hymn, yum, sniff—after which they began to meld, one into another.

When the cows all came to the top of the High Field, it became hard to make out anything else. I felt they were all around me—as if I were in danger of being stepped on. And I could sense the swaying provoking passivity of them; I wanted to startle them with a shout or a shot, as I had when a boy.

We had an arrangement over water: I asked Olwyn for a little more, then buried my arms beneath the sheets; she replaced the empty teacup on my bedside table at some point during the next five minutes, then gave a distant cough to let me know the gift was there. I said, "Thank you." She said nothing.

No—a lie—my senses moved slowly but simultaneously all into all, until time had no markers for its passage and I couldn't any longer tell which from what or how from who.

Only a teacupful, never more than a teacupful; with a saucer that was thin and cold enough to be bone china. A fairytale cup for a hut in the woods.

The smells begin to fuzz or clang out the sounds—the sounds which are acrid or chewy.

A cup of water tastes only of one's current annoyances; Gift.

Senses start: The visions I had were of loud feasts of plum, vanilla, tangerine and peppermint—all washed down with cool tremulous draughts of liqueurs dripped from slick stalagmites into bowls of velvet and crepuscule. Swimming through frogspawn.

Mmmm, in their forms I tasted Saturday or perhaps the long etched blue of Wednesdays between four and bells go one-two-faraway-three.

When I swallowed, it was the buzz of bees that tumbled down my oesophagus, to fill my watchful stomach with heavy gold and honeyed viola-tones.

That first week, I heard daybreak turn from smoky grey to lemonade to itchycoo.

My fingers run across the bitterwseet edge of Mozart's famous Piano Concerto in Pink Minor.

Kandinsky fills my nose with the taste of rainbows, non-equilateral triangles, oranges and lemons.

There was a name for this state, I knew, but I had temporarily forgotten the word.

One had the feeling that really one wasn't there—and that something else, something inhuman or unhuman, had crept or glided in and taken one's place. It wasn't disconcerting because nothing was present which was in any way capable of feeling disconcerted. Instead, there was an overall and abiding sensation of escape-thrill. One's responsibility for doing/being had evaporated. All that one was left with were the many, of which one was

more than all, one was simultaneously each and every—
creeping, gliding, lying, anythinging.

Within time I found kinds of time that I was sure had
not been there before.

Holes: it's not as if one fell through them, more as if
one were them, were holes, feeling constantly fallen-
through.

Because I could not see my self, I found I had no proof
that I was not invisible, and soon I began to believe I
was.

Very soon after beginning to believe I was invisible, I
began to fear that after all I might not be.

Once I began to fear I was not invisible, I started to look
for logical reasons why I might still be a creature of the
sun.

As I found no way of proving I was not invisible, I began
to behave as if I were—behave, although I was unable to
get out of bed—behave mentally, as I was still unable to
get out of bed.

I am no longer sure whether we are ever asleep.

Then I did get out of bed.

Then I was moving down the bed, as if part of me was
part of a slide-rule and another part of me was another
part.

The movement was smooth, mechanical, metallic, and reminded me of abduction, of being wheeled on trolleys with rubber wheels.

Was this on night six or day seven?

One gets the feeling one has spent a great deal of one's life, more than one actually remembers, being pushed along-over smooth shiny floors on soft rubber wheels; horizontal.

I was out over the end of the bed, impossibly; there was nothing but air beneath me to support me.

I panicked, was back in my body; it began again, another way. (Obviously, I had not liked that method of exit.)

The world tipped, and the bed beneath one was now behind one and one was no longer lying on it but merely leaning against it.

I repeat: One was horizontal without weighing down on the bed; one was vertical although one's feet were resting on nothing but air.

I tried to walk away from the wall-bed, knowing my feet were resting on nothing but air, and I found myself not taking a step, only moving forwards which was upwards but which felt outwards—

Through the open doorway, the deep, rumbling throb.

My body was behind me, no longer beneath me; my body was no longer my body—I had no control over it.

You try to move an arm, you fail.

You try to move your head, move it just an inch, you fail.

You try to clench your fist, you fail.

I felt myself falling forwards, pivoting around my ankles, as the room again righted itself. I thought I would smash my nose on the floor, but there was nothing there—and I was upright, head in the eaves.

Then I descended to the ground, unfloaty, like I was in a slowing elevator.

A gentleman should never condescend to condescend.

Then I floated down to the floor, unmechanical, like I was a flippant moonwalker.

My feet rested at ground level but did not put any weight on the ground; I did not weigh anything.

The deep, rumbling throb of the Lancaster bombers.

Then I was overcome by the fact that I could see. My eyes were still sewn shut. The room was filled with spillage of moonlight. I was still lying down. Olwyn— my captor, my saviour—was, I saw, sleeping in a Windsor chair over beside the fireplace. I was still still. I saw details I had not ever seen before, verifiable details: I saw the lines on Olwyn's neck. She was old.

Overall, the room—there was only one room—was overfull of detail. It would have taken a quarter of an hour to read the labels on all the glass bottles. And against the back wall, opposite the windows and the door, was a large, long, bulky object on heavy legs. It had drawer after drawer after drawer with brass handles. If I wasn't mistaken, this looked remarkably like a card-index—but surely couldn't be.

When I thought of being somewhere else in the room, I found I was already there—even before I'd made the decision to concentrate on going there.

The room seemed doubly moonlit, as my eyes felt more quicksilver than ever before.

But then the deep, rumbling throb stopped and started, stopped and started.

Moon-movement was like an exaggerated version of wishful reality: Think of it only to find it has already been done for you.

Grasses poked out of jamjars all along the windowsill, beyond my reach.

The throb came through the door and miaowed.

I could see the right hand side of every object in the room, as if each had been sharpened by a moonblade. So much glass.

If I had tipped my head to the right—if I had had a head to tip—it would have looked as if someone had sprinkled bright quicklime over every object in the room; camp.

All of a sudden, the scrunch of claws arriving.

Even with the sound-effects, I thought Olwyn might be throwing a carcass on the bed.

> As I was about to think of Olwyn, I found myself already in front of Olwyn; before I'd made the decision closely to inspect her, I was peering at her detailed surfaces up close.

Hairy face in my face; damp dabs against my cheeks; whisker-tickles: not a rat.

I had wished for a cat to stroke. Here were two. Tabby or not.

> I describe Olwyn, unfairly: Her heavy head was laid back, and both her eyes were covered by the crook of her right arm. She was an old woman.

For them to be live presences!—after all the death I'd seen; animal-empty Europe, only rats in the camp, only dogs around the perimeter, only silver-sliced seagulls as we flew over the Belgian coast.

If rats had come—playful—to be stroked, one could not have helped but adore them; planet.

Whilst all cats may be the same in the dark, they are quite distinct when one merely has one's eyes sewn shut.

The two cats had different presences, the one from the other—soft was anxious, rougher was a calmative; I don't know how it would have been had only a single cat had come. In other words, did they offset one another? Would soft have given me a heart-attack? Would rougher have made me comatose?

Describe Olwyn: What was exposed was her breastbone —and I could see the river-from-satellite wrinkle-forms upon it.

The cats restored me to time. Some frames are worth far more than the pictures they display.

The thud-thud of the one cat paw-licking on the counterpane.

Cats involve one, even against one's will, in a sensual world of silk-soft sullenness; perpetual mistresses. Even abandoned in the desert, they would still reside in the boudoir.

Especially-especially what I liked to feel was the drying of the damp dabs left by the cats as they cleaned the corners of their eyes against my knuckles.

Close enough up, a cat licking itself sounds like a mountain dividing.

I could tell the way I stroked them was annoying to the cats, but it wasn't until later that I was to learn exactly why.

Pad of dab of cat paws, departing, like a spillage of water drops in a room two rooms distant.

Then cat-face in my face: they loved to be in extreme close-up—I don't think they wanted to smell me, just feel they couldn't be ignored.

Sometimes I went beneath the covers, to escape the
cats, and they padded over me, like friendly prods from
a fat-fingered half-wit.

Olwyn woke up and looked at me, and I woke up and
found myself blind.

Indolence isn't something I've ever found easy.

Usually doing follows doing follows doing.

Enforced indolence was the only kind which really
existed for me—illness, sickness, hangover, the early
days of an affair with a woman who turned out to be
lazy (usually, I lost interest in her, because of this, and
went off with someone more active).

It was in the camp, or so one has been coming to
believe, that one learnt how to languish without
anguish, to recline and not repine.

Pour myself out into the dreamy cream-time of the day.
This was the first frist.

My movements, I would have said, had begun to
change—my fingers disported themselves more daintily
above the blankets; and now that I could not watch
them, watch them was exactly what I wanted to do. Just
sit and observe the simple movements of my wonderful
hands.

I have now been here for one week, and I am becoming
another person who is also myself.

It is possible to lead and live an entirely physical life—cripple, *coma sapiens*, Morris dancer, cop, cyclist—it is done by some; I had been looking forward to constructing my life so I never had to do this.

War-clouds: Each of my closed eyes was like a long nail driven up through my consciousness and into the hard specifics of where and when I was.

Along the windowsill I itemized at least five different varieties of dust: ethereal dust or dust-of-dust which moves before you ever touch it, but which you can sense because of its elusiveness; ash dust from the fire, which slides like graphite into the ridges of one's finger pads; skin dust (my favourite) which in large enough quantities is rollable; vegetable dust, stalky, which prickles back if pressed hard (larger cellulose than this would be splinters); grit dust, which crumbling plaster devolves to, and which perhaps shouldn't properly be called dust: it can be mouth-blown but does not air-waft.

Occasionally I thought of my knife, sleeping in that hole in the bottom of the tree, beneath the roots.

As I stroke him, the tomcat's ears snicker against my fingers as he twizzles his head.

If I were the last man left alive, there are very few things I could reconstruct, and most of the laws of physics would die with me; I am no encyclopedia on legs, but I have heard there is a weak force as well as a strong one—whatever that might mean. Some things are particles and some waves and some are both, wibble-wobble.

I lay there trying to picture exactly how one tied one's shoelaces—terrified I might forget.

There are things I know I should know, such as which toadstools to eat and which to save as poison. There are other things I do not know how I came to know, such as skateboards and personal computers and Ribena and discothèques. There is a war. The Second World War.

Olwyn has no radio; Olwyn's house had no reception; yet even if Olwyn had lived beneath the Crystal Palace transmitter, she would not have had a radio.

One missed the myriad beeps one normally ignores; insects are no real substitute.

Snail-moves: One missed music so deeply that one was forced to accept oneself as a passable Figaro.

Insects are more irksome than interesting—we pay them closest attention just before and just after killing them.

What one most wants to hear, in 1942, is that particular sound: 1969: expensive electric guitars coming through cheap, overdriven amplifiers.

To my left, as far as I can stretch, there is nothing but the wooden Windsor chair upon which my bitter drinks and sweet food are silently deposited.

I hear the ft-ft-ft of stitches being unpicked; little stitches, not eye-stitches; Olwyn-sounds. I hear scissors repeating the first syllable of their name.

At points, the birdsong seems familiar—certain passages of unlikely syncopation—and one begins to wonder whether it is a series of recordings being played in a loop: the same day, over and over again.

ft-ft-ft: One might hazard that one's parachute had flown hither from yon. A witch could do that.

All I really know is I find myself here and I have certain memories from before, none of them particularly con- vincing, many of them embarrassing, several of them it seems involving Adolf Hitler; memories which may or may not be memories; and that is all, sir, that is all.

If you ever have yearned to be a ghost, you deserve to be compelled into a ghoul.

It will be broken; I don't know how much more of this this place can stand.

So appalled by one's youth that one finds oneself inca- pable of experiencing it—except as the state of being appalled.

I did try to engage Olywn in conversation, often.

Thank goodness for the inventions of the blackbird— always *quelque chose de nouveaux*.

A gentleman should seem to lack nothing.

The thoughts of an invisible man are inherently conservative.

The past is a sketch, the present a painting, the future a return to paper-making.

One had the feeling that somehow one was being invisibly maintained—maintained in a steady state by occult forces.

It is difficult to live—impasto, chiaroscuro, wet—in a preliminary sketch.

I continued to be ashamed of the beard; to grow a beard is always to admit some kind of moral defeat.

Note: I can bring myself to the point of ejaculation but am unable to produce even the most trivial amount of semen.

Olwyn carries some obscure burden of gloom—she seems almost unable to go through with the simplest actions; breathing bores her.

Masturbation is a bit like buying oneself a birthday present—one knows one is going the be pleased-ish with what one gets, but there's never any chance of surprise.

Then Olwyn washed something, outside, probably some clothes.

By this time, I have stopped crying in pain and frustration.

My ankle feels much, much better, almost as if I hadn't ever injured it. Olwyn re-does the poultice each night as I sleep—I am sure of it; I confirm it later.

Why would there be a card-index here, I wondered. How might it have been brought here?

Olwyn sighed and baked bread, and I asked her to bring me the loaf; I sat there for half an hour, as it cooled, my fingers drumming on the full-hollow base of it. Heaven.

One knows that, here, one could have been a little less than happy, a little more than content; once.

Lobe-tract: Summer is an ecstasy from which every-thing feels itself to be the only thing excluded.

There were beauties to behold, though I did not under-stand them enough to witness them—not to begin with, anyway.

Where there is no illness, there is no true king.

. . as if the whole horizon in my hands, as if . . .

Mainly like distant, evenly dispersed stars of green against a night sky that has been mixed fifty-fifty with fresh red human blood; discothèque.

The gigantic kettle I could hear boiling, beyond the hill, that was the London train.

Welcome to the fewer-fever-witnesses; glistery.

I heard the witch washing herself. I heard the bubbles in the water as it boiled. I heard the ring of the tin bath on the hard floor. I heard the water splashing, and tried to tell what shapes it was splashing from, what textures.

The night is that of 1942; it is not that of later decades. I feel stuck in molasses, when I wake up to blackness, thickness, deadness.

Why not live? Why not?

I was convinced I knew the places on their bodies that cats like to be stroked (a cat can also be stroked not on its body, metaphysically stroked): the nubs in front of their eyes, egg-cuppy; the fin-ridges at the backs of their heads, flanging out, run your two forefingers between them; the hollow between the bones of their jaws, as approached from below; of course of course along the length of their spines, but even in this I was slightly wrong.

The only things worth doing are the things that can't be done.

Only a cat really knows how cats like to be stroked. These are not proper cats.

I clap my hands, begin to sing—I must be festive or my soul will die.

If I could choose to hear any piece of music, it would not be loud overdriven electric guitars, it would be something I had never heard before, by Schubert. There is plenty of that—an appalling amount.

No performance, perpetual rehearsal; birdsong. This has something to do with your life, too.

You are about to enter the left wing of infinity.

The wood-pigeon, like artificial fibres being tightly rubbed, one against the other; fade.

"Open your eyes," she says, waking me up, early.

One night, an event—Olwyn gets me out of bed and has me hobble to behind the stove.

"I'm going to have a visitor," she said.

I ask her why I can't stay in the bed—I would be more comfortable there. The visitor would be more comfortable in a chair.

"Because it's the bed I need," Olwyn replied.

She won't say any more, however much I ask, only, "If you don't want to be caught, you'll keep quiet. He doesn't take long."

It is surprisingly comfortable behind the stove; the area seems to have been cleared out; it isn't damp; there is no draught; I worry that I will fall asleep and begin to snore.

Hide and seek was always my favourite party game— no-one else knew the secret passages behind the walls of the Great House.

Jingling in the middle distance; Olwyn's visitor arrives, limping.

I hear the heaviest clunk, wood bound by metal, and know it is his double-barrelled shotgun being placed within reach. Oh Christ—I know.

Olwyn's morning mutterings ended, and she said, "Open your eyes now, if you have any mind to."

Call him Gaiters: His true name is something I do not wish to write down, in case it gives him greater power over me. Keeper of game; keeper of the game.

Gaiters, who wears gaiters, is an appalling terror—no less so now I am an adult than when I was a child.

I hear the whippy unlacing of his gaiters; the creak of the oiled leather of his boots; the tinkle of his belt-buckle; the almost silent thud of his tweeds as they hit the floor.

I hear his breathing become gasping become swearing become praying.

Olwyn's voice is hoarse from not shouting. "Go on, you fool," she says, "open your eyes."

Then I hear all the sounds again, but in reverse; he is dressing.

Olwyn's visitor departs.

A sealed-dove: Unstitch them, I think.

Olwyn hobbles me back into the bed, which is warm. She allows me to be in contact with her; she trusts I will not attack her. Her smell is different. Her smell has changed.

I feel disgust.

"I can't," I said.

"You can," she says.

Olwyn hobbles me back into the bed, which is dry. She allows me to touch her; trusts I will not overpower her. Her hair is scratchy and not soft. Her hair is probably grey.

"Unstitch them," I say.

"They never were stitched," she said.

Olwyn hobbles me back into the bed, which smells of stale bread.

Olwyn scoffed—I heard her make a sound she knew could only be interpreted as a scoff.

"Your eyes never were stitched," is what she says. "Why should I go to that trouble?"

I wanted to disprove her, but I feared she might be right. How could she—sighted—be wrong? My fingers sought my eyelids, and found them to be without the edge-ridges that had been there before—that I suppose I had felt as being there before.

Olwyn says nothing, but goes out through the door. (I see enough to see the quick blur of her.) And I cry out to her, to come back; she does not.

"Are you all right?" I asked Olwyn, when I was back lying down again; warmer than I wanted to be.

I blinked—such a beautiful sensation that I immediately began to sob.

See, I've fallen through the moment's floor, then through the floor below.

Blinking is unnoticed self-caress.

And the membrane sliding slickly down over the eye; perfect fit.

The acorn going back into the cup, jumping back into the tree—as time goes backwards; them falling and flipping out, then back up again, over and over, each time all anew.

It is morning and it is still dark and I have a chance to witness the dark.

The world of Olwyn's house was crystallized as I tried to see my way to it through the flare and glare of tears.

It was eyes I wanted to see most of all, after I regained my sight, because of all objects eyes are the most spectacular.

But the dark smear of Olwyn had left quickly through the brighter dark of the door.

"Are you all right?" I ask her just before she leaves—out the door, off through The Darkenings, alone, but certainly not to follow Gaiters.

It is eyes I want to see most urgently, now I have regained my sight, because of all organs eyes are the most ravenous.

Perhaps five minutes later, my eyes were wide, but still I was not seeing well enough. Everything was in front of me, the whole long-guessed-at dreamed-over room, but the details were not registering—not going in, even though I was seeing as clearly as I ever had; I was seeing my seeing, too much; I was seeing sight; it was still too dark to see anything else.

I wanted to see that I was seen, to prove to myself I was seeable; on this point I still have some doubts, though not as far as Olwyn is concerned. She clearly sees me. Yet what if I am her particular ghost? This, surely—the isolation, the metaphysical abruption—is how that experience would play itself out.

A gentleman should never be seen to handle money, except in a brothel or a casino.

One may toy with the idea of being a ghost but what one will probably end up with is a ghoul's hard labour.

It begins, day, with the firm conviction that it hasn't yet begun.

There is no light and what light there is flocculates into moths which are not moths which interplex without cease.

I inhale lake waters and breathe out mountain clouds.

The floor becomes the ceiling, it must do because something limbless begins to crawl across it.

Early morning objects can at first be inhaled, then drunk, then eaten, and only when dawn is completed do they become something other than food; Turin.

I can hold up the sight of my hand and lift my eyes to receive it.

The limbless something reaches the doorway just as the first breeze enters.

At this exact moment, I must turn my head to the left and look at Olwyn's room.

The white porcelain bowl on the table seems to have been sung into existence by a dozen thrushes.

This is not soft light, this is soft matter being illuminated by just the same light as illuminates hard matter.

To my left is the wooden Windsor chair upon which my bitter drinks and sweet food were silently deposited.

To the right of the stove is the wood stack, logs that must burn fragrantly, spitting their sap, filling the hut with the scent of burning forests.

The windows which distract me from the room are beautiful in their mottlednesses—green with light.

And, over there, the far wall—that couldn't really be a card-index, could it? I would have to wait until the sun had risen further.

The windowpanes were an effect of spiders but the brick floor was the cause of the entire world's generosity.

And now this whole morning is seen as through and after a glass of very good, very cold Italian white wine.

The light tinkles back from soft-edged surfaces; the porcelain bowl brims as if with birdsong. Each object resonates with total certainty of placement—for an apple to be on a table makes it causal.

This world beautifully is too full of worlds comprehensively for one person desperately to dwell in it abstractly.

This little room is absolutely chockfull of things worth describing. It is also very dirty. There are so many glass jars, which are very dirty.

There is, in my immediate vicinity, nothing that requires electricity to function. There is an apple on the table.

Olwyn leaves me alone the whole day; I try to get up, but I am unable to. So I have time for what follows; time for this.

The summerlight in this room was a mottled mottledness—it came down through high moving leaves and then through ivied windows.

A foot-wide plane of dust-motes between myself and the rafters amuses me, until the sun goes in; I blow buffets through it, flushing and crumping they go, then I watch the familiar reconstruction of randomness.

It does not even strike me that, for the first time, I can be absolutely certain of where I am. From here, I can plan to go on with my mission.

Look at all the sparkly things in the air! They rotate in the sunbeam, as if finding the best position for their brightest halo—as if models at the end of a catwalk.

You watch them as they leave the light, but trying to pick them out after they cross is difficult, your eyes are so speckled by those in glory. You had forgotten there was such density of life, such fecundity in unremarkable spaces.

As a boy, I felt the dust motes needed to be defeated, and I thought I might achieve this by spitting on them. That was another lesson never learnt.

Brown shadows of evening totter into the room, drunk, Swedish, happy. And still Olwyn had not returned.

Olwyn had not returned right up until the moment she returned.

Whites, blues, greens, violets—face-tones.

Olwyn has come back to the far corner of the room, next to the stove.

I see a broad line of vertical light, straight down what I assume to be one side of the face.

Eyes, I think those are eyes, a little over five feet from the ground—one of them looks in a different direction from the other, slightly; they are slightly further apart than might be expected; they are a little darker than might have been anticipated: sometimes they seem almost as if they were all pupil.

Nothing is so obviously ambiguous as a mask.

Areas of her cheeks appear to have been cross-hatched whilst still wet by a vertical and horizontal comb.

Olwyn looks older than her voice sounded. I am disappointed; I had hoped she would be beautiful.

She was haggish—yes—admittedly—she looked like one should have expected her to look—leaf lodged in brittle hair, wrinkles not just around the eyes; witchward.

I try to isolate what is witchy about her, and fail. She is only as witchy as the next woman—and who would the next woman be? My mother. Ergo, Olwyn is witchy.

"You didn't sew my eyes shut, then," I said.

"Why, when I didn't need to?"

"But you pretended that you had," I think my tone here was accusatory; I don't know what I was trying to gain by this—her renewed animosity; to bring out some likeness to my mother. "You said you liked sewing."

Olwyn laughed more genuinely than I'd heard her laugh before. Then she began coughing, but tried to keep laughing, even though it was becoming a struggle.

"Yes," she said. "That is funny."

"And do you like sewing?" I ask, still trying to think of what her laughter reminded me of.

"Indeed I do like sewing, but eyelids aren't the easiest of things."

"So, you admit you have tried it before, then?"

"Oh," she said, "do be quiet now, and let me be."

Supper is made. Olwyn's unconsidered movements around the kitchen seem to be those of another person, younger, far less full of hate.

A set of emergent nails, pinkly, thickly.

I have seen no evidence that Olwyn is a witch; apart, perhaps, from the jamjars full of whatever they are full of.

Olwyn makes soup and brings it to me.

When she comes towards me it is for a reason, but when she goes away it is for a purpose.

Although Olwyn's eyebrows did not seem in any way plucked, they did seem shaped—only some kind of attention could have achieved such a balance of form and wildness.

There in the middle of her nose is not even the slightest of bumps; no warts, no moles, many-many wrinkles.

I would say she was sixty years old, depending on how hard her life has been. Living in a wood, perhaps she was only fifty-five.

She was not thin. Her stomach has its appurtenances.

Olwyn, at this time, would not look in my direction, let alone at me, let alone into the focus of my face.

"I have done just about everything," Olwyn says, about half an hour after the last talk of any sort.

To force a woman or man or child to behold you, a defi-
nition of rape?

On the first day of the second week, I am able to sit up.
My knife.

I did not yet know the colour of Olwyn's eyes, beyond
the guess at very dark; eventually, I found they are the
colour of wood—mahogany in the half-light, walnut in
the rarity of sunshine. To say they shine as if beneath a
servant-polished varnish would make her sound duplici-
tous, so I will have to say it.

The place is not simply a dirty place; I have come to
believe that a great deal of its structural integrity is
dependent upon accumulations of dust, dirt, refuse and
binding grime.

The camp was a very different kind of dirty—that was
communal, military muck, this is personal, expressive
grime.

Olwyn's hands have a mahogany sheen of dirt that
has polished itself against other dirt and against dirty
cloth. It would take more than a shower to change her
colour—I think only a week of Turkish baths, of the
sort only available in Turkey, would begin to do
something.

I wondered how Olwyn had become so expert at the
manufacture of dust, and especially in its intersection
with the light-effects of the sun passing from one set of
windows to the blank back wall. Does she put effort
into making her hut a certain kind of Mitteleuropean
grim? As if each particle of dust has, at its centre, a core
not just of darkening soot but of leadening angst.

I feel I know her hands have been upon me; marks.

That moment of summer inattention when the evening flicks from lighter-than-seems-possible to darker-than-seems-fair.

We were not meant to be as clean as Americans, but we were not meant to be as dirty as this.

If Olwyn sleeps, and I sometimes doubt she does, it is on the low chair beside the stove; I have turfed her out of her bed, though she says she only ever uses it during the summer. The cot-bed is too close to the large window, that's the problem with it. "I should move it to be right in front of the stove," she says.

> On the second day of the second week, I am able to move to the Windsor chair. My knife has a blade about five inches long.

There is no ticking here of clocks. This would annoy, some.

Olwyn seems sunk into almost total blackness or whiteness or blankness or whatness. To move, for her, seems to be to risk disturbing a wasp's nest of agonies. She seems to begrudge time its very existence, and to blame me for everything that happens to happen. The wasps in her nest are not merely skin-stingers but as soul-painful as suicides. Her time is pure deathly grind, this is easy to see. And every time I in my time open my mouth to speak—to speak what?—another suicide flies out.

And all of a sudden, nothing happened.

My eye-moth: As the day ends, the light-patterns
beneath the leaf canopy go cheetah, leopard, puma,
panther.

On the third day of the third week, I am able to move
the Windsor chair towards the door. If my knife could
speak, it would scream.

We are obvious, like dirt.

When the fire dies down, we begin to shiver—even in
August, even now.

On the fourth day of the second week, I have been here
eleven days. There is leather around the handle that
goes into dark brown crumbs when the knife gets wet.

The light switch, isn't—just isn't; here. When late dusk
comes, we pass moment by moment into a blacker and
blacker air; floccultation of darks; until thoroughly
envelveted.

I wouldn't have believed there were so many moths.
This, if anything, convinces me I am in an England
before extreme pesticides.

Naturally enough, I wanted to climb the tree from
which I had fallen—into which I had fallen; I wanted to
see if I had left behind in it any trace of my passage.

Naturally enough, I wanted to retrieve my knife.

Soft distant rhythmic hissing, travelling further in the
dark; the London train, the London train; qualm.

I stand up and go to the table and pick up an apple and put it down again and go back to bed and lie down again, feeling as if I had journeyed to India and become extremely unwell.

At first I ventured no further than the Windsor and back. But after a few days, as my ankle gained strength, I made it to the doorway and from there to the Lloyd Loom chair in Olwyn's garden. This did not consist of flowerbeds full of blooms.

A slant of moonlight coming through the close trees; enough to display the spider's web, but not itself the spider.

Outside: Of my love, my great love—it is a rare-rare chance I have to write directly of this speckled island; champions-who-almost-always-lose.

Nature had no nationalism, but Flora had her favourites—and England was always her eye-child.

French trees always look like they are getting ready for an inspection; German trees, like they have just passed an inspection; English trees, like they have just heard their inspector has died.

Among the birds but amid the insects, I sat—feeling the native rhythms pass through me; it wasn't tone, it was timbre. If I could only prosecute anyone who didn't feel the same exultation.

The cold flannel against my face, only the night air.

Olywn had cultivated the woods nearby her house—
though it took me another day before I noticed how
carefully it had all been done.

Concentration upon the details of Nature is analgesic—
and the smaller the creature, the greater the dosage. I
had once cured the toothache by following an ant
carrying a breadcrumb.

Olwyn's was the gardening which conceals gardening.

I lay down, and constructed a small pile of breadcrumbs
into a light pyramid beside my left eye, then watched as
the ants discovered and then dismantled and distributed
it. What had been a vertical triangle turned into a
wavering horizontal line. After this, I thought of the
individual morsels, being taken each one under-
ground—eaten, digested, used as energy, used for
growth. If I could have been entirely consumed by ants,
I might have quite liked to die, then and there. But there
were flies around also, who would get to me first—I
would be maggoty before I could be useful.

The cats were my constant companions. When I sat in
the Windsor chair, they sat in my lap. When I lay down
by the breadcrumbs, they lay down on my legs.

The woodsmoke smell, even when outside in the wood,
several steps away from the cottage.

Cats and man have this in common, I wonder if . . .

The witch's morning absence is her trip to the well, to
fetch the day's ringing bucket.

To say "Curiosity killed the cat" is to mean "Kill your desire for knowledge"; if your desire for knowledge isn't potentially suicidal, though, it isn't true desire, and what you're after isn't truly knowledge.

Out of nowhere: The nightjar chirring like something that has yet to be invented.

My adrenalized hands shaking so much they are useless, and all I've done is go for a walk around the house.

A canopy of branches hung a safe distance above the chimney stack, helping to disperse the smoke from her fireplace.

One of Olywn's cultivations was to create an approach to the house wide enough that she didn't bump against a tree trunk or trip over a tree root. There was a clear path, but it made a zigzag approach as it neared the front door. In this way, no-one ever caught accidental sight of the house from afar off.

Although it was a relief to be out and about once more, what I most wanted was a glimpse of The House Beautiful. I felt I would be able to tell, from certain signs, whether my grandfather was at home or not. When he went up to town, the place wore a completely different air—it smelled of cigarettes. The chauffeur would be absent, but the second butler would sit on a deck chair outside the kitchen door. Sheets would be hung out to dry among the topiary of the formal garden, where they caught the best light. If it was a quiet day, no wind, I would be able to hear laughter through opened windows from the girls cleaning the house. When my grandfather was in winter residence, the shutters would all be closed. When my grandfather was in residence, the house went into a form of mourning.

Curiosity only killed the cat if what the cat was curious about wasn't death.

The ground had been paved with the flatter parts of pebbles—some only as big as a tuppenny bit. This must have taken Olwyn months. The stones were mainly flint, so must have journeyed some distance to where they had upended up. Later, I imagined midnight flights of beach-plunder to Brighton or Shingle Street.

Whilst the witch was out, on the morning of the fifth day of the second week, I swept the floor of her cottage. When she came back, she did not seem to notice, and if she did she didn't say anything; I was not yet a presence. Or I did not think I was.

One still did not believe one was in the domain or lair of a witch. Her luxurious hovel was a complex of simples. The light split itself into rainbow-forms through refracting and reflecting glass; thick lemonade bottles with frosty marbles of glass in the bottom, to disturb the peely dregs. Stems of inexplicable straw stuck out from behind a row of blue tinctures—gum arabic, containing hemlock. The vitrines were organized by virtue of colour—the lightest at the top, down through green and indigo to shiny olive black at the bottom. Where the contents were white, in clear glass, they touched the fretted roof; desiccated slices of pale lemon, grapefruit, lime and orange; root ginger, looking like it would grow on anything, even human flesh; red berries were lower still, though, as they aged and darkened they would descend even further towards the floor;

hawthorns shrivelled like too-long-bathed toes; rowan-berries and rosehips I recognized like friends; the labia-like edges of certain rare mushrooms; black roots.

When someone is gone, it doesn't matter how far away they are, they are equally gone whether they are next door or in Australia.

I waited that morning—the sixth day of the second week—until Olwyn had gone, then I went.

I had retrieved none of my clothes, though I searched the house with all the thoroughness that time allowed; it was a card-index; that was the black silk of the parachute.

Being conscious of being naked as I walked, I felt I had nothing in common with primitive man. I wished particularly for my floppy shoes.

Barefoot I tread on twigs but they feel soft. I know which are the soft twigs on which to tread.

The Darkenings had changed since the last time I remembered being there. The trees seemed to grow more densely, heavily. I was able to maintain my pride in knowing the place, however. I could still find my way. Or, The Return of the Native.

Squirrelesque: a waveform of fur up the diagonal arc of a branch.

A robin makes straight short flights away from me, branch to branch, deeper into the holly bush.

I am looking out most of all for Gaiters the
Gamekeeper. He terrifies.

In daylight as in moonlight, the tallest oak tree; canopy.

Tree-climbing—I found it hard to believe this was once
my greatest pleasure.

It's not that we get worse at climbing as we grow older,
it's that the trees become less inclined to help us; they
prefer children in their boughs.

Tree-climbing is a vertical dance with a gang of petrified
octopuses.

Tree-climbing—I find it hard to believe I had forgotten
how great a pleasure it is.

A few feet off the ground and one already can't believe
what one has achieved, and by such simple means.

The risen-above world is a suddenly-breathing place.

I associate any altitude with the smell of three different
kinds of engine oil.

Through the imaginary spyglass, from the top of the
oak tree, I see The House Beautiful; hang.

Leisure: The House Beautiful is approached in the time-
honoured way of English country residences, along a
winding road with an innate but understated sense of
drama. Only at the very last moment does the tall brick
façade flash into view—even for one who grew up
there, and has driven some extremely fast cars along

that approach, the moment of vision always comes a few seconds after it is expected. Perhaps the hedgerows, with all the gardeners off in Aden and Mons, Casablanca and the Pacific—perhaps they have grown beyond their wonted height. Eight tall chimneys rise above the central portion of the house. The gardens were landscaped by someone no-one has ever heard of who wasn't called Capability. Tall windows look out towards a green slope of lawn, a low fence and then miles and miles of flatness. The hill here is the highest point between England and Moscow.

A gentleman—English—should reassure foreigners of his bona fides by appearing to be nothing more than a parody of an English gentleman; this is particularly important with the French.

There's nothing quite like an architectural masterwork to spoil the view.

Pylons, on the other hand . . .

If that bloody great house hadn't been in the way, this would have made quite a pleasing prospect: mostly lion-flank fields of clay-grown wheat, in the middle and middle-distance of which appear the chimneys of the brickworks; tall, gradually tapering, too far off for one to read the white-painted downwards letters. And in the far North, the town.

. . towers of spiderish form, and a genuinely positive contribution to the English landscape.

The elements are simple and familiar enough. The grass is light green, the trees are dark green, the wheat is golden, the sky is whatever colour the sky is that day. But, come evening, colours will appear that have never been successfully recorded. To call them mere browns is wrong. They are amber and russet, sepia and umber, ochre and chocolate, dovethroat and mist.

Those overhead wires with their perpetual x'xxx'xx.

I sit in the branches of the tree, gazing Northwards. If I live, this house will be mine. The view would be better without it; the world would be better without me. These two things might still be simultaneously accomplished; that is what I believe.

Inked: As the wind gusts, the light-patterns beneath the oak tree go leopard to tiger then back.

Wherever I have been, I've carried a photograph of this view with me, in my head's wallet.

The breeze shifted the branch like a cat landing on a mattress, tinily. Is this who I would want to be?

If one gives them enough time, trees can say almost anything; most of what they come out with is astonishingly positive: they don't even seem to mind— all that much—being felled.

It wasn't etiquette so much as worship.

I wish there were a pair of binoculars, dangling by a leather strap from the highest branch.

Most of all I should like to blow up a bright pink balloon; pylons.

With my knife, I return to Olwyn's house.

Could I be said to have been kindled by my being there?

The cats rejoin me at the door of Olwyn's house, although I am sure they have watched me the whole way.

Olwyn has returned, there is fresh water; Olwyn has departed, there is no Olwyn.

I examine my knife very carefully, then hide it beneath the mattress, against the wall.

The cats, too, examined my knife very carefully. They looked at it as if it were a fish—which, in a way, it is: a fish that swims through time.

I will go to the house right this moment, and so I would have done had not Olwyn walked in just then and begun making tea. I knew I would get a cup, although she would not offer one.

It was as if she wasn't old but was wearing an old person.

There is a Green Man carved into the wood of the leg of Olwyn's table, but no pictures of faces on her walls.

Whilst in her close company, he felt nostalgic—because her woodsmoke-in-wool smell was the smell of his childhood memories.

I lie down and I get up; I get up and I lie down. She pays little attention; she is never in my way.

A sparrow came and landed on my knee whilst I was asleep; I flinched and it flew off—and when I woke, I had a sense of having missed something.

I have time to watch the tree-shadows, leaning reddening into blue—and I know I will have time to watch it all again, the following evening. Time enough for this.

How much is patriotism buffing the greenery, polishing the beetle-backs, plumping up the berries?

The soldier in me was less contented than I would have wished him to be.

These are flora I looked up at from toddling legs, had picked as primary bouquets, ignored as a little soldier (except when they offered cover) then thrashed for self-punishment when an adolescent. I know how exactly their stems crack, shatter or hold together. I know which grasses slip tasty stems from long sheaths, suitable for nibbling. I know the dangerous and enlivening mushrooms. I know how to stroke nettles without getting stung.

I wanted to march—I wanted to march as well as I did before.

My life, into this book, these notes.

"Where is my commanding officer?" I think. "I need to be told what to do."

Olwyn groans before she moves, and mutters at herself for groaning.

Two weeks ago, we were on the parade ground. My body had been capable of as-one-marching, capable of goose-stepping, of maintaining a tempo that would kill new recruits. I thought about what I had once been able to take part in, and would probably be unable ever to take part in again. It was the fulfilment of my life, in some ways, to be one of a troop, all moving in exactly the same way—as if my demand of my knee that it raise were obeyed by the knee of a corporal eighteen rows behind me—a fellow soldier I would never personally know. But it was when furthest into the collective, into an almost mystical state of communal oneness, that I felt the purest form of individuality. These moments gave me a basis from which to judge the remainder of my life. I knew I did not think the same thoughts as the other men—although their thoughts at that moment might have been similar, or the same. They, too, might have been burnishing the sheen of their own selfhoods. This was the military form of meditation—force considering itself—and what always brought it to true beauty was the inspecting eye. With this in place, the soldier could ignore all external reality. The soldier's eyes were open, wide open, but for this sound was the greater sense. To be square in the footfall, loud in the crunch of an about turn. He wanted, more than anything, to empower the rhythm of the singular men around him. This mission made him miss the simple life of a soldier. To die in step. He was marching, now—in his head, he was beginning to understand the beauty of his training: his body would obey commands not given by himself but only relayed. In this, he became stronger than he should have been. Because the battalion operated through him, he brought to bear the force of the battalion. Their collective will not only supported but became his will. And yet, whenever he wanted, he could feel his isolation. Alienation and invisibility were alike only a thought away. The battalion was capable of anything. If they had been ordered on the parade ground to levitate, he was sure they would have done it. Every day they obeyed orders without knowing what they did, or how.

Along the near edge of the cornfield runs a four-stranded barbed-wire fence; I know the places where the ground dips, making rollunderable gaps.

Splendid these excuses we offer for not only our weaknesses but our triumphs!

The English—unable to cope with anything greater than the day-to-day, the humdrum, the monotone.

Always engaged in our constant and unceasing Quest for Cosy!

If we win this war, it will only be so that we can sit down and drink our tea and eat our cake undisturbed for the next thirty or forty years.

Would you have the Lion burst forth from the caretaker?

The games mistress kaboom into the unicorn, of which she was always capable?

Then just you come and spill our bloody tea, why don't you?

This is Hitler's view. According to my memories.

When Hitler has a view. According to my memories.

The points of the barbs are these days about as sharp as
the claws of a lapdog; they could scar your cheek, if you
employed them as tools to that end.

> I sleep and when I wake, my clothes are sitting on the
> Windsor chair, as if waiting for me; my boots are on the
> floor beneath, as if they were my purpose. The clothes
> have been washed; the boots have not been polished.

> Here, red, a blaring eruption-interruption of red—
> crimson, if that weren't to overdo; my entire visual field
> to become an instant May Day Parade in celebration of
> Marxism–Leninism, by red-skinned comrades with eyes
> like red snooker balls. So healthy! The whole sponta-
> neous demonstration is full of nearly indistinguishable
> marching movements. Flags are waved. Banners are
> lifted. One is impressed, as one is meant to be. It is as if
> I have already joined. If one could only become this
> exact colour then all one's troubles would dissolve. We
> offer you another kind of time, comrade.

> You will have met the Führer long before you meet the
> Führer—we all have, haven't we?

> So I have my orders; I have just been delayed by incapacity.
> The propulsion of doubt, again.

Fenceposts splitting along the lines of their coarse grey
grain, and twisting down towards briar-shapes.

> I wake up cold, as if in an October tent—not cold as in
> the Camp, which was as if in a good larder.

The air around the bed needs movement before I can
enter it; I blow breaths. Growing up in an old house, I
assume I am used to this; I wave my arms above the
sheet, like a scarecrow conducting an orchestra.

As I think of it now, I realize that—in the camp—I
missed this barbed-wire fence quite as much as I missed
my grandfather.

> Today, I am recovered enough to do something
> more than climb a tree. Today, I may dress myself
> appropriately.

> What shines here shines there also.

Rolling under the fence, I should feel myself crossing
back from identity to respectability; of course, I do not.

We develop so constantly, so radically, to become so
unexpectedly the thing we originally were.

> Wisdom sleeps while you blink.

I walk the grass path down the small slope to the not-
quite-yellow wheat.

My childhood is an ivory-inlaid box that can only be
opened by that magic key, cliché.

> Wisdom is a minute younger than Hunger.

The wheatfield, after the wood, felt like the space in
front of an aerodrome.

Everything in the universe apart from oneself was
utterly fascist, in the true sense.

One was convinced that—if one looked—one would
find swastikas instead of spots on the shells of ladybirds.

Rabbits don't usually giggle and shout "Jahwhol" as they
run away from one, do they?

> Look, the decision-monster, riding through its own
> crimson!

If one were to dig, one knows one would only reach
down as far as the layer of buried spades.

I don't know why I thought I could just walk across the
cornfield and into the house.

I could no more not go than I could not breathe; perhaps the whole mission can be achieved easily, in a day,
in an hour.

The five-bar fence in the hedge.

To enter a garden is always to become the voice of the
LORD God.

I would believe in it more completely were the lawn not
camomile.

An overgrown garden is paradise, when it belongs to
someone else.

Neither Coventry nor Dresden could offer a clearer
illustration of the sorrow and the pity. Never had I seen

the lawn this unkempt; never had I known grass grow
with such abandon.

To see weeds ravishing these flowerbeds is, in its way, as
disturbing as seeing one's best chum tortured.

I wish at this moment, as I set off, I were feverish—that
would give me some excuse for what follows.

It is not me walking towards the house, it is the house
sliding towards me; the fact my feet are moving is
irrelevant.

If only I could execute my grandfather now, I would
never become heir to all this gross needfulness.

The fear of the fear of the fear; it must be this that sets
the heart a-beat before the heart has reason.

The leaves glutting the basins of the fountains—which
yet still gush—must have been filmed a dozen years ago
in black and white.

The waters flow down from the hill above, are woken
by the fountain, descend to the ornamental lake and
thence—by way of a pipe—into a common stream; after
that, they are no concern of ours.

I had never understood the form of the fountains—
three vomiting unicorns.

From The House Beautiful, voices.

The purpose of gravel is to advertise sinister footfalls. If this is not the case, why does it do this so much better than anything else?

Crouch down behind a tree; listen to the breathing of the gun-carrying man—listen until you think you might live.

If there were a sheep-pen, I would shelter there.

The man who limps past will be Gaiters, the game-keeper.

A gentleman should never appear utterly entranced by anything other than a horse or his fiancée on the day their engagement is announced.

Gaiters limps past; he is evil, has always hated me—I still won't name him, because that would give him power.

Although those preceding and following it are hellish, the specific moment terror turns to panic is a blessed relief.

What would the best of all possible foxes do?

The Gamekeeper did not break his stride, not any more than his stride was always broken, yet I knew he had sensed my presence.

I myself am hiding inside a topiary bush; before it out-grew, it would have been the shape of a rabbit.

If they knew you as a baby, all it takes is anger to trans-form a person back into a giant.

The Gamekeeper lives in the Gamekeeper's lodge and tortures poachers.

Although this—my bower—used to be a large topiary rabbit, since the gardeners all went off to be blown to pieces it has itself grown to resemble something more like an explosion.

The Gamekeeper could not go off to this war because several parts of the Gamekeeper did not return from the last one.

He smells me, that must be what it is; he smells me and pretends he hasn't smelled me. The Gamekeeper enters the kennels and I hear him talking to the hounds. I am almost certain I hear him saying my name.

When I gulp, my Adam's apple seems to bring up half my stomach acid with it. What would the best of all possible foxes do?

I make a dash for the house, just as Gaiters comes out of the kennels. He hadn't smelled me, probably, but now he sees me, plain. Does he recognize me? Immediately, he turns back into the kennels. Immediately, I know what he is going to do—a limping man cannot catch me. He needs help. There are few other men around.

Strangely, I had a plan—I had always had a plan, not only because this scenario had been a recurrent nightmare of my boyhood, but also because I had anticipated its possibility ever since being given the mission; ginger biscuits.

I couldn't just lead the pack back to Olwyn's hut—I had to try the thing. I knew I would almost certainly fail: water, climbing.

As a boy I had delighted in being able to pick out certain hounds from the mass by voice alone. Now I listened to the pack as a whole, and it seemed a repulsive thing.

I ran towards not away from the house.

There was a pipe we dived through, out from the ornamental lake to the river—once, a man got stuck in it; a drunk man; boys slid through. Could I? Could I?

Dog-sounds are always hopeful; even the worst of their whimpering ends in a question mark. "This will stop, won't it? You will stop, won't you?"

Through the side door, the kitchen, the parlour, slamming doors behind me. Out the larder window—that would bottleneck the pack for a few minutes.

If there had been more able-bodied men around, I should have been caught instantly.

Sometimes, when one is running, one seems to overtake oneself, and then one has to redouble one's efforts in order not to be left behind.

Generalization is a privilege of the sedentary; those running for their lives tend to deal only in brute specifics. Foxes are most usually empiricists.

Called Woofer, Whisper-Boar, Watercourser, Waiter, Tripper, Trigger, Tigger, Tiger, Sweeper, Streaker,

Stiffener, Sleeper, Slaver, Shifter, Roger-Roger, Roarer,
Ranger, Punter, Porter, Poker, Nigger, Neighbour,
Nagger, Masker, Musker, Lurcher, Light-tower, Leaper,
Kinder, Jongleur, Jangler, Incher, Hun-Catcher, Grrr,
Gunner, Fetcher, Etcher, Dreamer, Destroyer, Courser,
Corsair, Conifer, Charger, Cauliflower, Catcher,
Brooker, Bounder, Boocher, Bolster, Bitter,
Beachcomber, Astor.

When running downhill, one realizes one has only an
approximate notion how long one's legs are.

I think about chickens; I do not want my final thoughts
to be of chickens; perhaps one really is on the point of
turning into fox.

Even as a boy, I had always given a symbolic laugh when
I jumped off the ha-ha.

I wish I had leisure to observe the herons on the margin
of the lake—one, two, three of them, elegant, verdigris.

The hounds have been ordered from the house, and
now they come after me, tumbling like a forming-cloud
rolling down a sloping hillside.

This is not a paperchase.

The pipe is slimy on the inside; the hounds will not
follow.

None of the hounds will follow through here. How
long before they pick up my trail?

Down to the bottom of the lake—not the swimming-bottom, the compass bottom; South. There was an out-flow pipe. The hounds were back now on the scent. Their voices went up in excitement, sounded as if they were being part-strangled. The water was sucked away towards a small river which had no name. It was close to the Eastern edge of The Darkenings. Through the pipe—if I went through the pipe, the hounds wouldn't follow me—no-one would. To go through was suicidal madness; to go through was my ultimate boyhood self-dare. I was still fairly sure that I would fit through.

Smooth with weed, sliding through, not knowing—I remembered; I remembered the terror.

Swimming through frogspawn: swimming through tad-poles: swimming through frogs: swimming through myself.

Head, goes beneath the surface of the green water.

Into the pipe, swept now.

Then I swam into antlers, charging towards me; that was my first thought.

It was as if a stag had charged me from the opposite direction.

Stopped; trapped. It didn't matter whether I was near the end of the tunnel, midway or just inside. The flowing water flowing wouldn't let me back. I was being pushed into the points of the antlers, which were slimy and could be bent quite easily.

Ten seconds I had been stuck, perhaps; perhaps not even that, but they were death; bad.

Bubbles caught by clothes against my chest tickled out along the length of my arms, getting more and more delicious as they went. Like one was taking a bath in champagne.

I did not stop thinking—green water flowing past me—I do not stop thinking—green waters past—what I thought was unexpected, was sad, was this: it wasn't Olwyn as she is but Olwyn as if she were a mother, as if she were—green waters—nursing a baby. What I felt in my thought was green grief that I would never be the father of that impossible child; whatever happened, drown or not, I would never father that child.

Mud-clumps I had stirred up with my feet continued for a while to slide past me, then the water began to flow clear; this was more deathly, less interfered with. I would become just another obstruction; not a flailer, a bad fish.

(A sudden certainty—I wouldn't die, I couldn't die and even if I did it didn't matter. This immediately followed by a greater certainty: I would die—I was terrified of dying.) I piss in the flowing water.

The crown of my head touched the slimy roof of the pipe—and I found the shudder of this reassuring: I still had the time to feel disgust; I still had possible lives of further disgust to live.

The antlers bend against my chest. One lies across my face. I can feel them giving way. There is no stag-bulk behind them. With hands that are mine but feel like many more than two, and far more powerful than human, I begin to twist and rend the antlers.

My eyes had not been open; they had been screwed tight as if re-sewn: now I glimpsed, in dying desperation, that light was ahead of me—close—through . . . It was a bush—I was wrestling with a thorn bush—some unwritten biblical parable.

There was a frenzy in me—I became a frenzy of fast and hard movements—and the antlers began to give, torn away from their grip on the soft pipe edge.

I cannot breathe and I don't mind and I cannot breathe and I do mind and I cannot breathe and I fear death and I surface to the sound of hounds.

Olwyn was standing at the sink, washing clothes; hers.

Into the air and the light we slid, the tree crown and myself, recognizing that what I embraced was a tree crown and not a stag's head—into the light and air and sound of sounds.

From the far side, I could hear the hounds giving tongue. It was a melody I had always wished I could love more than I did. (My bedroom overlooked—over-listened—the kennels.) And now that I knew I should hate it, I began to see its beauty—the collective was after me, and each individual hound was only a wave within the surge of the tide.

Horses, too; I can hear the thud of horses.

I might have died, drowned; I had definitely lost time; I could not allow myself the luxury of relief.

Pushing away the tree crown, it sank, so waterlogged and reed-heavy it was. As the antlers submerged themselves beneath the green surface I again became convinced my opponent had been a water-stag, fashioned of branches, reeds, weed and pure hatred of mankind. Mighty adversary.

Bloody pond weed!—like I'm carrying a drowned Old English Sheepdog on my back.

Horses galloping on the land.

running and I'm running and I'm running and I'm

From the hounds from the horses from the gaiters. Charging through the woods, I . . .

When I arrived through the door, Olwyn was there.

Bleeding from the hands, from the inner wrists; these are not paper cuts; Easter wounds.

Birds I do not hear continue to sing.

I jump over roots that would otherwise have tripped me, fatally; I am excited that I am not tripped. The Darkenings are a place I know.

I have seen the hounds' ambling sprint before—from a parallel ridge, from horseback—I know that they always look as if they could go much faster; I know that they can go like this for half a day. The hounds have very wise legs.

We did indeed look at each other, Olwyn and I—almost as if we had the time to do so.

The house came in sight, smoke at the chimney, door open—awaiting us.

If the hounds catch me, they will not kill me; they will injure me in proportion to my attempts to escape—until their master, Gaiters, is with them. It's not as if the pack hasn't been used before on a tattered man.

Olwyn could hear the hounds; I didn't need to speak to tell her what was happening.

The hounds if they caught me would stand above me, snarling, like a grove of trees in a gale.

My next significant sight, at bay, would be the gaiters.

She stood and time passed and the hounds drew closer and a decision seemed to be made.

Olwyn opens the door of the stove and, as she does so, says, "Undress."

Not defeat; not yet.

Love: I had no idea on what basis the decision was made.

Without hesitating, he did as she told him to.

If Olwyn's house had been another quarter mile away, I would not make it. Through the trees, beneath the branches.

The door is closed, bolted; my trousers are almost off . . .

My clothes and boots went into the fire: Olwyn pushed
them in further with the poker, put wood after,
kindling.

And then Olwyn sang as she attacked me—it felt like
that; she was pushing my head down, pressuring the
neck, making the vertebrae click: I felt lighter, manipu-
lated; my toes began to curl forwards of their own
accord; I sneezed, becoming softer; Olwyn's angry fingers reached my nose as she chanted and puttied it for a
moment, sticking her thumbnail in a couple of times—
new breathing: the room was getting larger, and Olwyn
had me up off the floor, losing weight, my bones emp-
tying out: I started to say something, but she stroked
my long throat and it became a different sound. Lo, I
was thunder-voiced.

Hound-nails were scratching on the door. Hound-
nostrils snuffled along the bottom edge.

All I was—when I ran into the house—was ragged desperate breath-upon-breath and a body trying desperately to save the person who might one day return to it.

The hooves of the horses made everything quiver,
landing as if directly on my heart.

The room darkened as their raised forms outside cast
shadows across the windows.

Panic: Inside one is an infinitely regressing tunnel along
which an infinite line of versions of oneself is sprinting,
in the attempt to burst out of and overtake one.

The hounds were loud enough to be in the room, it seemed. Olwyn reached behind my anus and tugged my coccyx out into a line of expression. I knew I was plastic; I knew I was becoming her animal: I thought I knew which animal. My ears were tweaked and pulled onto the top of my furry head; list.

Olwyn held me up, my spine in an inverted-U, so flexible.

"Not my best, but you'll do"—she said. "Now, go with the others and hide."

There almost wasn't a moment when I realized that this was proof of Olwyn witchery.

As the door was kicked and kicked, I ran under the bed.

The door splintered and one man two men three men entered—to find Olwyn and three dog-terrified cats.

Olwyn was there, Olwyn was, at the sink, almost as if waiting.

The man who only clearly becomes Gaiters as he begins to speak asks, "Where is he?"

As if someone else were inside me, vomiting or pretending to be an injured earthworm. I was still breathless.

"Who?" replied Olwyn, and gave him no more help than that.

Learn: The other two cats pushed back and back into the dark; they were better at making themselves small than I was.

"You'll send someone today to mend that," said Olwyn of the door.

"Where is he?" Gaiters asks.

All I can see of him is all he is.

"Who?" Olwyn repeated.

Men began to search the room, destructively.

The hounds were sniffing under the edge of the bed, a few feet away from our cat-hiss-bundle. I feared they might, with their strong necks, flip away our protection. But with two mattresses on it, and all the blankets and feathery pillows, the bed was heavy enough.

"My cats aren't sport," said Olwyn. "Call off your dogs."

There was a wait.

Some of the hounds leapt in the air to bark—they were detecting the black silk stowed up in the eaves. Gaiters ignored them, focusing on Olwyn, and so missed out on finding proof of my presence.

"Call off your dogs, or I will speak to your master about you."

The nose-huffs and dripping teeth of the hounds were whistled away—only to outside; we could still hear them.

In a moment the light brightened as the bed tipped up and we three were revealed—the Gamekeeper, the

Stable Lad and a man I did not know looking down at us.

I could not believe my form had changed, even though my eyes were impossibly close to the ground, even though I saw everything quite differently; language remained.

No-one thinks to look in the stove, so certain had they been of catching me alive.

Wouldn't Gaiters recognize me, even as another creature? Wouldn't his hate alert him?

Tiger: I transformed my face into an ancient Chinese mask, forcing it into the correct shape to make me feel the things I needed to feel—warrior-emotions.

A picture of me would not have appeared out of place spray-painted on the bonnet of a hot-rod: circle of inward-facing teeth, slit-eyes, bristling whiskers.

Absolutist instant: I had control of every hair of myself, or so it seemed, and there were many many.

We three were spitting up at him as he spat at us, once.

"What did you expect to find?" Olwyn asks. "Do you think I keep men under my bed?"

"No," said Gaiters, "You make them far more comfortable than that."

"Clear on out," said Olwyn.

The bed fell down on top of us with a crash like the commencement of a thunderstorm.

Horses trotting away—the trees are too close and the boughs too low for them to gallop.

The hound-voices never seemed to get any further off, although they had apparently been departing for five minutes; reign.

I was still being searched for by others, but Olwyn knew where to find me.

"You know I am put out," said Olwyn-the-giantess, "and you shall stay as you are until I have made up my mind what—what to do."

She opened the door to the stove and pulled my unburned unharmed clothes with the poker from the fiery depths. They were not singed, neither were they warm. They had passed through the realm of magic; where nothing is ever changed unless meant to be changed.

I crept back into the dark and the warm, and warm and dark sent me to sleep. Thereafter, I had a righteous superslumber of the type that hadn't overtaken me for years.

When I wake up, it is of course from a nightmare of being turned into a cat; my circumflex spine horrifies me; I hiss like water beneath a kettle on a stove.

I made a straight line, out from beneath the bed. Olwyn was in the chair.

I had no idea how long she would keep me catty-captured. I didn't know whether she would be able to turn me back again, and I had no way of asking. But she did speak to me, as she stroked me. "Calm down," she said, "calm, calm. Stay here," she said.

Being stroked by Olwyn: Rembrandt / Niagara Falls.

As I licked myself for the first time, I discovered that I was a dusty tortoiseshell the colour of sultanas, raisins, currants—in fact, a tortoiseshell that matched very nearly the interior of a Christmas cake.

My tongue told me that I still had all my teeth, only sharper.

This is a vaster, more accessible world.

I crawled into spaces smaller than those in which, as a man, I would store my shoes.

A large cache of mouseheads is discovered beneath the card-index.

Cats are to their homes as diplomats to their host countries.

I didn't know whether Olwyn the witch would or could change me back—and to begin with I didn't much care.

Like the aristocracy, cats respond only to nicknames, never to titles.

We three cats sit outside, listening to the gay twittering of the menu.

Birdsong is so delicious.

Sunshine, it became like water to me; cats can't keep diaries.

I would go to the cornfield and discover mice; my body knew how to hunt for me.

A gentleman should, when he is in the country, kill something larger than a squirrel at least once a day.

To sport a blood moustache and take a feather bath—satiation if not contentment; contentment would have been the achievement of perpetual killing.

It's true, I enjoyed killing all those mice: I couldn't be expected not to kill them, I was a cat; I couldn't be expected not to torture them, I was a cat.

So unlike the human who must also torture but must also feel guilty for being an animal who can't torture without feeling guilt.

I even enjoyed fake waltzing on the kitchen floor with their little stiff corpses. How they would slide and roll and even flip between one paw and the other! When I brought one in, Olwyn was always proudly dismayed.

For a cat, desecration is glorification—and the longer it goes on, the more profoundly reverent it is. The unworthy are eaten, snip-snap-snorem.

If I could, I would have spent the whole day killing—if I had been a king-cat, able to have solider-cats bring me a perpetual supply of sweetly-pissing-themselves-even-more-than-usual mice.

Cats have no music, no music to anyone but other horny cats. At midnight one found oneself mewling in moon-mottled nettles.

I don't really like milk but I seem to be addicted to it. When it arrives in the concentrically ringed blue-and-white bowl, I run towards it—even though I have been promising myself the liberty to distain only a few instants before.

The moon is patient with my impatience; she takes a closer, colder look each night.

I could bully myself with my tongue—it was almost rough enough to kill a mouse.

A cat speaks with its spine.

In terms of human physical eloquence, my spine had gone from foot to hand.

My mission was still there.

Miaowing was little more than the equivalent of shouting, "Hey, you up there! Look at my spine!"

The first time I did a corkscrew pivot as I fell, I couldn't believe that one end of my spine was facing up and the other—having twisted through 360 degrees—was also facing up. I then wanted the witch to turn me into an owl, so I could experience a head that was able to rotate through 360 degrees.

A tail is a physical second chance, a fall-catcher, a twist-achiever—though if one uses it correctly, those second chances should only very rarely be required.

The witch was canny; she read my spine as if it were Torah and she were a Rabbi.

Olwyn's intuition, when it came to the mysteries of cats and to my mysteries in particular, was quite remarkable. Here was a form of language greater than speech, dealing in gnosis rather than exegesis. My wish was more than her command, it was more even than her wish—my wish was her being. Which did not mean that my wish, whatever it might be, would be granted. I knew at least that it had been refused out of self-denial as much as self-assertion.

For example, I straightened and lengthened my spine, running my claws into something applicable—the red velvet curtains of cosiness—to announce that I was going out and wouldn't be back for quite some time.

And, best of all for a cat, she knew exactly when to leave me be—which was almost all of the itchless time. When I did need assistance, with a flea or a flea-bite, I would make sideways jumps as I wrapped my spine around her leg.

From the moment I dived out of the Douglas Dakota to the moment the U-boat rose to collect me, I had been destined—so I had thought—to be entirely on my own.

I do not expect to have a single proper conversation—not unless I gut-shoot Winston and then tell him, in detail, all the things he would have accomplished but now never will.

The house was still there.

In answer to a posture, Olwyn reassured me, "I will keep you this way for a while—just a few days, don't worry—until they are no longer suspicious. Until I've decided what to do with you. You'll be cheaper and easier to feed than a man. Hungry man."

Her skin appears to have been removed, scrunched up, slept on by elephants and then put back as it was before.

The Nobel Prize. The Iron Curtain. The bad water-colours.

The moon waxes; the wheat ripens; Olwyn ages; fingernails.

My grandfather was still there.

I claw my sharpens against vertical wood.

It should be that only a cat knows how a cat likes to be stroked.

My knife was still there.

Pour myself out into the creamy dream-time of the day.

The difference between happiness and contentment is that between resting and being at one's leisure.

My mission remembered, even in cat-form, I decided to reconnoitre The House Beautiful.

At noon I set off through the thick wheat—mistakenly assuming no-one would be about. But this being neither Rangoon nor Bangkok, both the Englishmen and the mad dogs were about.

Judgement has no place in Eden, only in the expulsion therefrom.

Olwyn could not have seen me go—she was off and away somewhere or other.

What man ever went better disguised? What cat ever had a better motive for creeping?

The moment one thinks one's happiness complete, one's happiness ends.

Nothing is so tritely ambiguous as a mask.

I could not resist that sweet field mouse, encountered halfway across the field, even though I left his top half uneaten—his ribcage open, like a wasp-bitten strawberry.

I walked beneath the pylon in the middle of the field. Its erection had been one of the consternations of my childhood. Without it, I would not now love the place so.

Those wires had gone crickety-crick over my adolescence, bringing the summer airs to a shimmer, making the air crackle like bacon in boiling lard.

All idylls have always seemed as unreal to me as Tennyson's of the King; even ones I myself have experienced.

I am moving purely forwards, at this moment, at this moment.

Propellers; Today it feels as if I will knock something over that will later brim with blood.

But for home, there was nowhere now for him to go.

We walk towards our blood.

I will not be purified until I have made of the dust a second gift.

We walk through our blood.

I was almost across to the other side, the fence, the lawn, when I heard my first danger.

Sizzling, the house cats, Thomasina and Tabitha, tried to chase me off—but I was more immediately violent than them. A decent scratch to the flank of Tabitha and my path was cleared.

It was laundry day, the most opportune time, those who were not extremely busy were off and away—up in town, dealing with bookies, gunsmiths and vintners

Yet I knew, by not focussing upon it, by deliberately bracketing it away from consideration, that my time as a cat was idyllic.

My childhood is a tortoiseshell box inlaid with mother-of-pearl that can only be opened by a silver key. At leisure now, I walked around to the front door, up stone steps, and found it wide open.

To enter a garden at dawn is to be corrupted.

My parents were not the sort of people one met without first making an appointment.

A home where, when one came across it in a corridor, one would step around if not actually over the body of a dead dog.

One could surely not have grown up here and still turned out as one has? Miaow.

My childhood is the property of an inexistent identical twin from who I was cruelly not separated at birth.

A gentleman should never confuse superiority with nobility.

Enter the library, speak to the past: "You are too rich to involve yourself with hand-to-hand combat," he said, in an earlier argument. "And you are just the sort of son that will get himself killed. Imagine what your mother would be like to live with if that happened. Weeks of tears, weeks and weeks. I'd have to have her sedated, if not hospitalized to get her out of the place. Be sensible. Get yourself a job at the Home Office or the BBC. Go and work in propaganda. You're good at lying." And then, soon enough, my mother had ceased to be any kind of excuse.

Fatherland: The house, seen through cat's-eyes, was more like that remembered from my childhood than the house I had walked away from to enlist. (None of the servants would disobey my grandfather so much as to give me a lift to the station.)

Faces forming from the walls; of course I imagined imagining this; self-spooking, so as to get maximum value for money. But no pockets.

The clocks in the house—grandfathers, grandmothers—there are clocks, but a cat can't tell the time.

A familiar voice: Every definitive statement is an embryonic fascism.

My grandfather was a man of manifold distrusts, all of which he viewed as part of my inheritance.

The past of the house began to speak. (This cannot be, because I am a cat; and I have still not sorted out what kind of language possesses me.)

I have always taken my grandfather's warnings as recommendations; all my girlfriends have been Celts.

His monstrously comprehensive incomprehension: my grandfather's.

It comes as a list, all elements of which are read simultaneously; I do not purr; Rat.

Distrust anyone who doesn't smell of sweat, dogs or horses.

Distrust anyone who makes frequent use of the word "exquisite".

Distrust anyone who would gain from one's death.

Distrust anyone who wouldn't benefit from one's success.

Distrust anyone whose accent secretly makes you want to giggle, except royalty.

Distrust anyone who believes in the abolition of the House of Lords.

Distrust anything wind-powered.

Distrust anyone who would not, if offered, turn down a seat in the House of Lords.

Distrust compassion.

Distrust anything that runs on three wheels.

Distrust any man who looks even remotely like Jesus Christ Our Lord.

Distrust anyone who confides in the Vicar.

Distrust any man who volunteers too eagerly to buy the first round.

Distrust anyone who doesn't recognize the importance of having heard the first cuckoo.

Distrust anyone who doesn't own a landscape painting in oils.

Distrust anyone who refers to one by one's first name, except immediately after a funeral.

Distrust anyone who has read Proust in the original, especially if they are French.

Distrust anyone who claims they knew Picasso but not very well.

Distrust anyone who wishes to discuss the means by which their mother fed them up to the age of fifteen.

Fodder: Distrust anyone who has undergone any form of psychoanalysis or who takes vitamin supplements—they amount to the same weakness.

Distrust men who say they love their infant children.

Distrust anyone whose hair touches their collar.

Distrust anyone with "a general philosophy of life".

Distrust any enterprise that requires new underclothes.

Distrust George Bernard Shaw, specifically.

Distrust aphorisms. (He never said this—he never said any of these words—because for him aphorisms came under the category of the exquisite.)

Distrust typewritten letters.

Distrust Jews and photographers.

Distrust anyone who believes their heritage is Celtic; in fact, it's probably safest just to have them shot.

Distrust anyone who doesn't naturally know how to take a good photograph.

Distrust Buddhists, they have nothing to lose.

Distrust water.

Trust fire.

Trust dogs and horses.

Trust both your hands equally, and trust the corner of your eye.

Trust the smell of grass but only when it has not been new-mown.

Trust decisions made before breakfast; distrust decisions made after dinner.

Trust His Majesty the King, unless he is Her Majesty the Queen.

Trust British historians born at least half a century before Karl Marx. (Trust gentlemen.)

Trust Italian opera; distrust German opera; ignore Czech, Russian, English and French opera.

Trust Bach; distrust Mozart, except when he's obviously writing about death.

Trust the Lord—even if you can't quite bring yourself to believe in such a ridiculous entity, it's still worth seeing what it feels like to trust absolutely in something absolutely trustworthy. Trust other your Father.

There were further lessons to be learnt, but one was not the person to learn them; cat.

These would have to be my private, personal Proverbs of Hell.

The beginning of the middle: It takes me such a long time to recognize the importance of the card-index.

The walls were glistening eyes which tried to talk to me; simply.

The floor beneath my paws gave way because tar was beneath the carpets, or toffee.

The library is a long, narrow room—the bookshelves on either side seeming almost to close in above one's head.

I knew the whole house was edible, deadly poisonous.

I did not need to pass through the library in order to reach where I was going, but I wanted to see the library more than any other room. The library was where the murder was intended to take place.

My room was exactly the same—even the newspaper I had been reading the morning of my departure still lay across the counterpane, yellowed. My departure had been precipitate. Had the mice not had at them within minutes, my toastcrumbs would still have speckled the little roundtopped Sheraton beside the bedside.

On every surface, I smelled mice; this had become their domain. I also smelled my dead human self—I smelled lots of deadnesses, one on top of the other.

Curling up and sleeping; Of my cat-dream in my boy-hood bedroom, on my boyhood bed—say, bliss.

Later, I wished that I had been able to stay awake and, more than this, explore the room, go beneath the bed for the treasures there, mount the wardrobe and survey the dusty terrain; but I knew I had taken it in more completely in my dreamstate. The dimensions of the space, the acoustic particularities—echoes off the ceiling absorbed by the counterpane and the overstuffed armchair; rippling air along the red book-spines.

Ravens could arrive, or crows, or starlings, but rooks—
you have to admit—are grander.

As much as my grandfather loved his riding boots, so much did I lavish them with cat-piss.

Calcutta; I bouqueted with more than several anuses my grandfather's pillow.

A man came into his bedroom, heavy with distrust.

My whiskers twanged into harsh spikes, sharp as teeth; my muscles seemed to rebound at the oddest angles, like a thousand balls being fired around a fives court; my eyes saw so clearly they saw the physical future, just. I didn't so much hiss, I sizzled.

Some people live their lives as physical beings—athletes, dancers, wetnurses—but one had never been one of them; enforced.

Dogs make great entrances but atrocious exits; cats—in my opinion—vice versa.

I ran down the corridor as fast as I could, down the stairs, turned the corner and entered the library—still sprinting, aghast. At full speed I ran past Geography, The Classics, Erotica and Gardening Part One. The vanishing point got further and further away, as if it was being flushed down the lavatory and I were being airlifted out of the cubicle, out of the toilet block.

Olwyn is soon to be displeased with me—very displeased.

Breathing: As if the whole house had turned into a hunting animal, hunting itself.

They did not release all the hounds to chase me, just the fastest one, Incher.

Is there a question enrages a woman more than, "What do you want?"

Nothing is so infuriatingly ambiguous as a mask.

Surely just about anyone would stop doing just about anything to watch a dog chase a cat.

After the cat-incident: It's not just that she doesn't reply to me, it's that she refuses to acknowledge language exists.

Her two eyes, I am certain, exist only in two different universes; and unparallel.

My skeleton was desperate to escape my skin, and my nervous system wanted nothing to do with the blood sought by the dog.

Olwyn hears the commotion, and knows it must be me being chased again. Olwyn is right but wrong but right.

The corn stalks were thicker for me; I know this fast
dog, Incher, she likes killing.

Don't let your distilled thoughts spill from your head-of-
cup—they will, if you run too fast over uneven ground.

The dog is faster than me, though running for sport, not
life.

> I go through a gap in the hedge, the hound must run
> across to the five-bar gate.

Whilst it is chasing me, it is a dog; once I am safely up
the pylon, it reverts to being a hound.

Olwyn took her time, walking down from the hut to the
edge of The Darkenings—exactly as if she wanted to
teach me another lesson.

Her stomach has its own particular objections to me.

I was rescued by Olwyn, who sent the hound whimpering
away with a thorn in its paw.

A gentleman should walk as if he were being carried
and—if ever the circumstance arises—be carried as if he
were walking.

"Why'd you have to do such?" Olwyn asks, more herself
than the cat. "Why'd you always have to go and be so
silly?" She could swing the cat from its scruff, but
instead she lets it recline along her arm; indulgence. The
cat feels the soft woollen warmth of her breast along its
left flank.

At moments you are known to have exploded.

Outside the hut, in yellow sunshine. I could have been made a goldfinch and kept in a cage or a woodlouse in a matchbox, but Olwyn showed a strange mercy. (Olwyn has several birdcages, all empty, of course; Olwyn has a small wall of matchboxes.) I could not remain feline-form, she knew. I could not be trusted, she knew.

After the delightful tortoiseshell cat, which was intended to be hidden in plain view, calmly Olwyn ripped me apart into a baker's dozen of black rats—two of them pregnant with litters of twelve and fourteen respectively.

        I outran myself, became one's line of terror, fleeing;   streak.

When it could go no further, it went further.

The wisdom of animals bounces back off other animals; if it isn't emitted, it doesn't exist.

For Rats, one and another is one and the same.

The blossoming of the realizations that one's mouths are in extremely close proximity to one's mouths.

Ratness was like being a schoolboy again—no, it was like being an entire classroom of boys who have just been told their teacher isn't coming in today, and that they should study quietly. Riot!

Hard enough for retaining a sense of identity; some-times I caught myself looking at myself looking at myself from behind. "I"—pah!

Eyeball-into-eyeball contact is the scariest thing: I can stare deep into my own thirty-ninth of a rat-soul. And there isn't much to see there, I can tell you.

Dawdle, we did; dander—dwell and sometimes doss.

Rat to the power of rat: I was able to explore an object from many sides at once, smell it, nibble it—all of this making Analytic Cubism look like *Ceci n'est pas une pipe*.

My reflexes were appallingly great—a twig snapping half a mile away had us pissing ourselves—and when we felt one of oneselves beginning to get arthritis, we just let it take greater risks until, eventually, it made a mistake and died.

I was born, repeatedly, which was horrific—especially as I was, at the same moment, giving birth.

And a couple of me did die—one, drowned down a wellshaft and the other caught by a mongoose.

When compared with being born, dying was—Riot!—exquisitely pleasurable.

It's almost impossible for human language with its prissy pronouns to cope with rat-stories—rat-number-thirty-nine stories; there are many many things happening and all are happening at once and all of them are of life-and-death importance; we rats don't fuck around, even though we do—Riot!—spend a lot of time fucking around: One of me is over here on the bendy branch—wagging up and down—while the other finds some mushrooms and starts to eat while the other is trapped upside down in a hollow log and scrabbling

scrabbling panicked going to die until it topples over
because another of us has seen my tail and pushed me,
not to rescue me but just because I thought we might
have found something to eat while some others form an
arrowhead convoy direct across the ornamental lake—
scaring the Stable Lad, who runs off leaving us with his
baitbox.

Each Rats to see Rats as a backwards star.

Rats, yes, to go into-along tubes of good-air, foodward-air.

Rats, no, not to go into-along tubes of scare-air, death-air.

Rats to seek dimples of ground—gnaw—to feel her
belly up against her.

To move across silks, this to be very important for Rats;
most quasi.

Rats to have no young-Rats or old-Rats only fashionable-Rats and unfashionable-Rats.

Olwyn intended me to learn some humility: existence as a
pet for whom regular meals were provided was a privilege.

Rats to watch Rats for signs of incipient unfashionability.

Rat-being enduring was intended to tick me off for
misbehaving whilst a cat.

Fashionable-Rats to make rats only with fashionable-Rats,
and no Rats to make Rats with unfashionable-Rats.

After being the rat-tribe, I would return to human form
a better human; theory.

Rats to appreciate—graw—good tailoring, particularly seams.

Olwyn was wrong—the orgiastic life of starvation and appetite was the best holiday I ever had.

Summer was an easy time for feeding; and rather than return chastened, I came back a cocksure rapist with very bad table manners.

Bestial is Celestial.

One strange thing, perhaps worth remarking on—as a rat, I have no desire to visit The House Beautiful. We know it is the domain of dogs.

This, the moment I am unratted: Olwyn sings half-an-hour to gather us in, as if ready for a concert, then makes a riddled bundle into a hairy body covered in tails, pulls the tails out, one by one—shoves them through the belly-button to make entrails, smooths the pelt down to my skin.

"This is something for you to watch," Olwyn said. We had not yet gone back inside her hut, after my reassembly. I was constantly thinking: "Rats must have climbed a tree, to be seeing from so high up; Rats to jump down." My feet did not understand why they were so heavy on the ground. "Look up," said Olwyn. The sky was black.

Then the rooks arrive because the rooks arrive.

Rooks, overscribbled neck-birds; a bird only for supporting the rip of a beak-talon.

When I returned to my body, from being cat and rats, I found that my false tooth was gone, and all my tattoos were missing, all three of them; I felt less pure.

If I did not come from the future time to now, as I think I did, would these black birds make me feel so powerfully doomed; if I had not seen them in a horror movie? Movie and not film, you see—these things erupt, eruct.

The tooth had been lost when I fell out of a tree in The Darkenings aged eleven.

Them all having been burnt in the stove, when I reappeared as a pursued cat, I had no clothes—so over the course of three nights Olwyn stole me some undergarments, socks, cotton shirts and a thick grey suit from washing lines miles and miles away. She never told me to where she had flown, but I thought the grey lapels smelled briny. I did feel sorry for the bewildered wives and washerwomen; I tuned in, at a distance, to the morning's accusations and resentments.

My tattoos had been the names of (a) an unmodern instrument of torture, (b) the mains electricity current and (c) a portmanteau word consisting of the internal combustion engine and the seat of the emotions and intellect, plus unnecessary umlaut.

The room is darker now it has become the rook room. The whole Darkenings is darkened.

What clothes encourage is always deceitful.

The card-index is a beautiful thing. I am glad Olwyn has preserved it. What was she thinking of? Why had it been thrown out? What wood is it made of? It takes up quite a lot of room in her small cottage. There are no books here.

Clothes were invented so that people might betray one another; keeping warm has nothing to do with it.

They are on every branch, but in a ring around the house; not a one so much as flies over/across/above the roof.

Without clothes we may not be more virtuous but at least we are more humorous.

Olwyn does not explain why she turned me into rats, nor why she turned me back, nor why she has given me a thick grey suit but no shoes, nor why she so often leaves me alone.

Nudity negates tragedy.

The rookery is an alarm system; we lie in the middle of it, and it makes constant noise. As if some immense ancient wooden casket were being perpetually opened and closed—the croak of hinges immemorial. But it is a settled cacophony, because if ever a poacher approaches, or even a larger-than-usual animal, the rooks erupt, eruct.

Unless it is a corpse, a naked body is comic.

Civilization is whatever is the opposite of sunburnt genitalia.

A corpse is not tragic; a corpse is beneath tragic.

They form a halo around the house, and sleep is else-where; Loomer. The very air is bilious, inked.

The suit fitted me as well as any suit ever has—even the bespoke monstrosities for which my grandfather took me up to Savile Row.

If we could only see it, a suit is the most tragic costume.

A suit is a fate. A suit is a portable funeral; what is mourned is behind the zip.

I don't think I can define tragedy, but I know that if I had to attempt to define it whilst naked I would have stood even less chance.

Tragedy is the choice between either dying or becoming very very silly.

Or, perhaps, tragedy is the withdrawal of the choice between dying and becoming the silliest person anyone knows.

Who could be sillier than Coriolanus, other than Macbeth, just before he dies?

Who could be sillier than Macbeth other than Lear, before he dies?

The feathers of a rook all seem to be flying away from the bird they are doomed to carry.

Who could be sillier than Lear other than Othello, before?

After the unratting and suiting, Olwyn seems to want to talk—more than before.

Who could be sillier than Othello other than Hamlet, before?

We were sea-creatures beneath an oil-slick, as if The Darkenings had put on a bitumen sou'wester.

Hamlet is the high-point of European silliness.

I looked into the card-index. It seemed to be from a small regional library.

Hamlet puts on the suit, for everyone.

I looked at a few cards. The handwriting was unfamiliar, the Dewey Decimal system was in place.

Remember, ignorance.

The feathers of rooks are slaves. If only we could escape, they wish and wish, escape our loathsome bondage—yet when they try to fly, so do their masters; this being how rooks ascend: through dominion.

I feel I am not being granted permission not to feel melancholy.

Olwyn asked me what I could remember of the time before the camp.

Every rook had shouted itself hoarse at the gross injustice of having been born a rook.

When Olwyn is angry, not that she shouts, quite the
opposite, she gives one a headache.

Because it's expectoration, all the time, all around one,
he expects some rain of black bile.

It was a proletarian garment, my suit; I found traces of
lavender spikes and calyces in the pockets.

>At first I can remember very little of the time before the
>camp.

"Why have you dressed me in these clothes?"

"Your civilian clothes no longer exist," Olwyn reassures
me. "This time I let the flames burn them. You are not
to be trusted to go anywhere."

>At first I almost begin to suspect that the time before
>the camp did not exist.

When I had calmed down, I read a few of the cards
from the card-index, trying to find the title of a familiar
book, but they all seemed to be non-fiction.

The rooks sang like insecticide.

>Olwyn listens to my confusion, then tells me someone
>in the village has just died. The funeral was today.

>We know our memories are our memories because we
>remember remembering them before.

I sit outside, in the sun, in my suit, in The Darkenings,
in 1940.

"They are going to come looking for you," Olwyn said. "It would be very difficult for me to hide you here."

Olwyn asks me to wear my suit to sleep.

This rookery business is like being surrounded by pygmy drummers who play only by stabbing frogs.

I wear my suit to sleep.

Olwyn stays up, making something.

"Think about these things—by which I mean your past—when you have some time," she said. "You may find something comes back to you."

"I hate that I have to do this," she says.

Sometimes, in their various voices—rev and crump, shikkle and cough—the rooks are almost worth listening to; hate-jump.

I wake up to hear Olwyn making a speech I don't understand: "Look upon it as an exercise in trust. They're going to come back and search this place—it were better you weren't here. And where better than there? That's where they want you, anyway."

She has buried me in the graveyard whilst I slept, in a coffin, in my suit.

Before I wake up, I think that Olwyn's house is extremely dark—almost as dark as can be; after I wake up, I know that there are darker darks.

I have time to think about it all, now.

There was some screaming, at first, I would admit if pressed.

I am a landed English gentleman; never more so, in fact.

Six feet under is the moral high ground.

Agreed, one had never been in such a private place, but, truly, one had been in many, many more fine.

Prison bars seem merely silly, until they stand between one and life.

I ask Olwyn if she can silence the rooks, please, and she says I only had to ask, after which they are silent—that night.

I can picture the churchyard above me; the view is of green fields.

Being buried alive felt inexplicably familiar, until I paid attention to the word familiar.

Six feet beneath sandy earth, one still was under the impression passers-by would hear one if one screamed.

This—burial—had never been my worst particular nightmare; that had always been flames.

One screamed.

It is far from silent; it is far from peaceful: I am not sure whether the things I hear are things or not—birdsong, voices, footfalls, bells—and so I endure this perpetual racket of incertitude.

For an Englishman, a place is a place exactly because of its ignored deaths. All the buryings beneath our feet that we live in ignorance of but are structured by; all the other buryings-beneath we will perform.

I spend time wondering whose gravestone is above my head, or if I have nothing more than an unsettled pile of sandy earth. For the dead, it is a great comfort to know the exact plot in which they have been buried.

I believe at times the earth around me gongs, as if it were brass being struck and struck again by a great hammer; perhaps this is the peeling of the church bells.

I thought she had decided to leave me there permanently —so my only agency was to decide that I myself, not she, had decided I should die this way. It was a difficult logic to force, but I managed—with the help of my always-present suicidal impulses.

There is only one thing I can do—reason myself into a state where I believe committing suicide would be the best thing I can do, then I would wish to be exactly where I am, only dead, and that will happen soon enough.

I will starve before I suffocate before I submit to going mad.

The feathers of a rook are Israel in Egypt.

My only choice is to choose to have chosen exactly what has already happened.

I wondered how close I was to my mother's corpse. I wondered how close my mother's body was to me.

My great hope was a drowning flood.

It is a brittle-seeming world, this—until one has tried concertedly to shatter it.

I think of all the skeletons around me, and whether there is any difference between me and them.

I think of all the skeletons around me, think of them thinking of me, and decide that there is a difference.

Death is an inhuman festivity.

A gentleman should never go beneath ground level except when, once a year, inspecting the wine-cellars.

I was unable to sleep because I did not get tired. I wanted to touch the wood-exquisite of our banisters, and not for luck.

No particle: We are obvious, like dust.

Here I am, sequestered from my origin. But not in any particularly satisfying way.

In what state is England? We aren't losing, we're destroying. As fast as we can, together, we are pushing everything of value off the White Cliffs and into the Channel. The whole nation is shouldering their part of the shove. What we live on is merely what the tide brings back.

As Olwyn had promised, I now dead have time to think about what came before.

What we as a nation, myself included, are best at is self-betrayal.

In England I am the corpse, in Germany I was the gravedigger.

There are better things you could be doing with your time; your time is only your time because of the better things you are not doing with it.

If I were really to die here, it would make no difference to anyone else.

Waves: I realize that among the things I miss are things I have no idea how I know they exist.

I miss the reassurance of wrongheaded people around me doing exactly the same thing I am myself doing: Particles.

I miss fireworks—the way they smell more than the way they look.

I miss the clarty-mouth-feel of monosodium glutamate.

I miss receiving letters through the post.

I miss the-moment-before-this-moment's news.

I know I shall always miss train-travel train-travel train-travel travel-by-train travel-by-train; tickety-boo.

I miss zebras—for some reason I am unable to comprehend, I seem to miss them a great deal.

I miss the soft-centred chocolates I hoped someone else—an elderly female relative—would eat first.

I miss my enemies, all those people I thought I hated, all those whose growth repelled and sustained me. I could not name one of them.

I miss being clean—even if the Nazis didn't exist, they gave me access to as much bathwater as I wanted. There is still, in my smell, in the grave, an undertow of pond.

I miss buying things with cash in shops—not any particular goods, just the moment of exchange.

I miss the names of commercial products; I wish I could remember even just one. Hoover. Ribena.

I miss waiting, not knowing on any level what is going to happen.

I miss, I am ashamed to say, a very well-known brand of hamburger; Spot.

I miss marmalade and werewolves.

I miss computers and all they pretended to be able to do.

I miss contrails above me and chewing-gum stars on the pavements.

I miss the things I can feel I have forgotten.

I miss the traffic jams that force one to consider where exactly in life one is.

I miss the card-index.

I miss Winston Churchill being safely dead.

I miss lateness and greatness.

I miss a witch.

I miss the future—the future of the world more than my own future; War.

Annihilate all regret and you'll regret it.

You realized you thought about Olwyn more than you didn't think about Olwyn—that is what being down there meant to you.

I clap hands, begin to sing—I must be festive or my soul will die.

It's a wise man who refrains from refraining.

I don't believe we are good, because of what we want to do; every monster is well-intentioned. Wasn't I myself?

Do you despair? Only for one moment. Which moment? That moment, rising.

I think about Olwyn, and she appears different to me. Have I begun to understand her? No, you haven't.

Birdsong; back.

No, you haven't.

I belatedly realize I miss birdsong.

Impatience is the desire to make time flow backwards.

I have found myself thinking about the contents of the card-index.

One feels one has undersold one's earlier terror; sang froid: it was cold.

We bounce backwards off what we did not know we were going to hit.

After a short while even terror becomes tedious.

Responses to questions I did not yet realize I needed to ask, had been written.

You do not begin reading at the beginning. You begin at the top of this card, with this line; you read this sentence, and the sentence following, and then obediently read the next card before going back to the first card. That's what you do, believe me.

After this, you will turn back to the first card. Because before you make any decisions you must read all of this. It has been prepared for you, by you, more painstakingly than either of us can imagine. Be grateful; feel satisfied. There is no rush, although you hurry.

If I were to say anything to you, as you sneak a look at this card you're not meant to look at yet, it would be not to blame yourself for any of your past stupidities, and not to expect yourself to be any less stupid in the future. But, God, I am so immensely stupid.

Olwyn's tinkle and clatter in the far corner.

How distant is the applause, and how one hates oneself for anticipating it.

I see nothing but glass; I see nothing beyond the glass.

Nostalgia for past angers.

She wished to preserve me but she wished also to punish me; this past tense is false. If she was and will be then surely she is.

The cards of the upper branches, outside, being shuffled by the hands of the breeze.

Landed: This is abysmal.

I wish I were rats again, with my teeth.

Has Olwyn grown slightly taller? Or is it merely that she is standing straighter, taking fuller breaths.

Time must have lost all track of me.

At moments you are known to have imploded.

Looking at her is like looking at several bunches of flowers before they have been arranged; one cannot pretend the effect is entirely satisfying, yet one doesn't know that a finished display would be any the better.

Insects must have observed me as my eyes were being sewn shut.

Phrase: Olwyn had taken me in; I had been taken in by Olwyn.

The way Olwyn looked now, one might almost begin to find ways of finding her attractive.

Olwyn's face looks two ways, mainly. If her mouth is open, angry or animated, she looks like a bird of prey at sixty miles an hour six inches above a mouse; if she is comfortable, she looks like a cat after milk.

No, not a poem; a timer.

Olwyn's eyebrows are two black lines so resolute they become beautiful.

If you had asked me, I would have told you she was a different woman—the first woman's daughter.

Olwyn is now more erect of carriage, less shaky and shrill of voice; her skin glows with renewed health and her hair has stopped absorbing all the light around it.

She never looks at me straight on, when I am awake; stern.

My heart feels as if it were trying to beat for two bodies at once.

I clearly recall every detail of my youth; that is a lie—I have forgotten the importance of the questions I used to ask myself, because most of them have now been slain by answers:

"No, I will not."

"No, I cannot."

"No, she doesn't."

"No, she can't."

"No, they don't now, and they never will."

"Yes, unfortunately."

"Yes and no."

But these answers do not seem to apply to Olwyn. She evades everything, just as a good witch should.

Exhumed: From this point on, one is assured of a future.

"I am twice as alive as other men," I told Olwyn, to impress her.

I remember my foolish disappointment, the first time I opened my un-sewn-up eyes. (Remember the shapes the water was splashing from?) Admit it, disgust.

"One day all the pus inside me will leak out," I said.

I had seen her, then, without in any way looking at her.

Increased clarity of vision turns the grotesque beautiful and the beautiful grotesque, until either value becomes affected; inestimable unending increasing loneliness.

It was first of all in moments of inconsequence that I began to see how Olwyn might otherwise be. When at a task, she would forget my presence, her movements, which a minute before had been abrupt or near-clumsy would become moulded, tuneful.

Olwyn would be still then move abruptly then be still again then move flowingly, without pause, for an entire hour; the ultimate rhythm was only visible from the vantage point of a week later.

Olywn was not a woman one liked to see drudging. I wished her with me, up at The House Beautiful, with servants to launder for her, cater for her, offer her treats. She would not have stood this rich-life for more than a day, not for anything less than love. But at least there would have been that day's respite from the business of keeping a decent house in the middle of a wood.

Her hair is grey not blonde; her eyes are brown not blue; her figure is scrawny not slender. I itemize, yet I begin to idolize.

There is nothing more pleasurable than struggling valiantly against the inevitable joy.

There will come a point where you will know you have to kiss her. You will feel disgusted by this, as later you will feel disgusted by the fact you ever felt disgusted.

If Olwyn had been a man, I might have been able to speak to her more indirectly.

Increased clarity of vision renders the grotesque beautiful and the beautiful grotesque, until either value becomes silly.

If I had had anyone but Olwyn to talk to, I would have asked their advice as to how to approach her—not because I needed any guidance, but for the pleasure of sharing my anguish.

To seduce is to dig a tunnel through the air.

One knew that on certain days one would not be able to recognize her.

Embarrassment is anger at self-defeat. I wanted to abandon my mission. I wanted to forget my orders from the Hitler-witch, spend a year watching a year passing, and then another year checking to see what I'd missed the previous year. I wanted to become a charming naturalist whose diaries could be rediscovered around the year two thousand and ten. Those were the only Englishmen worth being—the green men.

Would she turn me into other animals? A dog? A hare? A sparrow?

"No," Olwyn said, "it takes too much work, too much energy. I won't be to do anything similar probably until around next May."

I am very grateful, I tried to say, with my spine.

"Show me," she replied, and I had to kiss her.

"At last," she says, and sighs. "Why do you make me wait?"

This is where the glee begins, admixed.

Merrily: "I shall never be what you would call a good-wife. I have always been about escaping that. What I shall be instead is pure variety. Sometimes I'll be hateful, because I can't prevent myself from loving that. Sometimes I shall trickle away. Sometimes I shall become you so completely that you won't be able to tell whether you are you or you are me being you."

The world was being coated with translucency; one perceived everything, or so it seemed, through a portable lens of extraordinary brightness. Water was more pellucid than ever—in Germany, it had been an iron soup; here, it was as if struck fresh from mountainsides by thirsty saints.

I know that what I feel is tenderness, rather than anything else, because I yearn for this feeling either to be stronger, so it assumes the dignity of pain-to-be-endured, or weaker, so it fades to the triviality of warmth.

One knows there is more pleasure in each moment's breath than one has ever allowed oneself to feel.

Despite the little language we used, we said a very great deal.

When I put my hand into the water bucket, I saw the hand I would have wanted to have—at other times, my body felt the least loveable thing about me. Underwater, I felt myself to be properly myself. Sex with Olywn would be immersion.

Merely to transcribe would be utterly to vandalize the memory, retrospectively and prospectively; we said things to each other: they were meaningful things— saturated with that particular time.

One did not have a heart, as such, and it was not capable of being broken, like songs say, and she was not the woman who could make this happen—so why did I feel so utterly banjaxed?

Something happened which could not happen; Olwyn.

She walked across and lay down beside me then entered through the door and walked across and lay down beside me.

She walks across to stroke my head at the same time as she is running out of the door; do not ask me how this is possible.

She is walking across to kiss me at the same time as she is running out of the door.

Finally, she was walking towards the door but immediately, without turning round, she was walking towards me. Her body, somehow, had just reversed itself—a face appearing through the spreading curtains of her hair, thumbs swapping themselves for little fingers, the backwards kick of a heel transformed into the forwards flick of a toe. It was so astounding one couldn't even speak the word, How?

"I may not be everything you imagined, but that's your imagination's fault, not mine."

A gentleman should be as fluent in the little language of love as in *le passé composé.*

There are days that just simply seem to happen to one, as if one deserved them; Brand.

Out of the window, the greenery was like wallpaper for a boudoir; as a boudoir apes a bower.

My tongue dissolves like sugar.

I am thinking things I do not think I usually think; lovely—skin—lovely—lined.

Youth, that already-falling blossom.

Found the word golden.

I feel as if she had handed me over to herself, as a key.

As if it were a simple, singular thing.

We talked about things I do not wish to record, because I remember them well enough.

Since Olwyn and I kissed, the birds seemed to have stopped singing; or at least, I could no longer hear them.

In her eyes however close I look I see no veins. They are almost all pupil.

The world has had quite enough of beauty, I am sure.

We mentally create woozy-time, so as to disorientate ourselves—and we timeslip away from where we feel we should be, yet the feel-spot always remains there, within, off-central, locked.

My two bodies feel as if they had only one heart between them.

Olwyn leaves me, for no apparent reason; weren't we happy? Were we too happy? Later.

I am wandering, inside myself.

"A great big beast of a thing," is what my grandfather would call the card-index, perhaps putting on a strong Scottish accent.

Itemize: From left to right, four drawers then a drawer-wide interlude of wood, then another four drawers; from top to bottom an unbroken run of four drawers—making thirty-two drawers in total.

And deep—when I reach for the furthest-back card, my elbow rests on the edge of the card at the front.

I count, I calculate: 18″ x 110 cards per inch x 32 drawers = 63,360 cards in total.

Only one drawer, the furthest to the left, the lowest down, is empty.

Death to an inhuman facility.

No, this is not only a card-index—all the cards have holes punched into their top edges; it must also be—you once realized—a computer programme, early.

Why do I take comfort in paper and ink?

Of that night, after Olwyn's return, nothing sayable,
except all that follows.

> I float outside into the twilight—if only that were liter-
> ally true. Once, I would like to fly.

> Olwyn's kindness. She could have flown in the air,
> grabbed my parachute.

> I hear scissors repeating the first syllable of their name.

> The rooks argue about why they are still arguing about
> whether or not it's worth arguing about what their orig-
> inal argument was.

> There is a line and we must not follow it.

> That I had been propelled into the oak tree, not blown by
> accidental winds. A deduction: Olwyn wanted the black
> silk, which she now has fashioned into undergarments.

> The undersides of the nettle-leaves looked as if they
> had been coated in milk, left to dry, and then veiled in
> spiderweb.

> Mankind is moonkind, as far as time is concerned; I
> used to be an exception, but I am not now.

> Wonderwood: It wasn't that I saw faces in the tree-bark
> trying to talk, there were faces trying to talk in the
> tree-bark.

We were together as we had not been before.

I am walking deeper into the depths of the wood.

A grove of silver birches, inexplicable, circular and in the very heart of The Darkenings; yet one knows that when one sits here one glitters with visibility.

I have a head full of a head full of Christmas.

There were juicy-shiny-leaved rhododendron bushes, which I would have wished elsewhere.

In the room's dark middle distance, undressing, she is like the left half of a pint of milk being poured out.

What shines there also shines here. My nostalgia for the neon I know I can never have seen.

The stars overhead are merely paste; the true diamonds are those reflected in a bucket.

Idolize: Nude with long hair.

The moon has been full, and I have missed it; buried.

I do not think I love her; I think I do not love her: I continue to be furiously curious about her.

It's not that we don't speak, it's that we refuse to acknowledge language exists.

Until I became a cat, I thought I knew how cats like to be stroked.

I go to where I can see The House Beautiful, light over water between the trees over corn.

Her kisses tasted like water that has been reboiled after cooling. This was a good thing.

Nothing is so truly ambiguous as a mask.

>The border between respectability and adventure is marked for me by barbed wire.

We bounce back off what doesn't absorb us.

The true delight of hide-and-seek is finding the hiding place where only one's love will come a-seeking.

We knew that we had never been here before, gladly, very gladly.

Not one single thing; never less than infinite.

>One shall return to where one was, and not even approximately.

I am so glad to be above ground that all I want to do is holiday in this sensation; breeze, light, Olwyn.

I did not realize until days after this how perfect all her faults were.

A gentleman should never admit to having dreams—his waking life should answer to all his desires.

Her cunt was a sunset viewed through brambles whilst lying on your side.

Of course, until this point I had only imagined this; I had never, not even as a cat, asked to see it.

A knot of pink flesh, like a tiny dangling foetus.

Fellatio is really by far the sweetest thing one human being can do for another.

That combination of slimy and granular, repulsive until it becomes the only true thing in existence.

The penis is womanish, and must often be wooed just as woman is wooed. But not in this case.

Wisdom is starlings, not owls.

Perpetually and perpetually intensifying pleasure, for whom could this not remain an ideal? Apart from every-one.

When it comes to sex, we are all—even the dutiful daughters—prodigal sons.

The cats are still around; they watch us at our love-making, curious, amused, trying to work out exactly how they might join in.

Embrace; honey-soaked toast; night.

It is impossible to kiss—to kiss properly, I mean—and at the same time to hear birdsong; the sea, though, augments.

Everything that wasn't Olwyn wasn't.

Sex, for women, is a hopeless business—about over-flooding an already-damp valley.

The feeling as my cock went inside her cunt was—
plastic, melting, stretching under its own weight as it
begins catching fire.

Consenting adults are the last people who should be
allowed to describe their sexual encounters.

To be comic: One wishes it were less like hyperventila-
tion and more like actual suffocation.

To transcribe is inevitably to traduce, but if we wish
there to be any kind of record we have no choice.

Armpit; pepperpot.

It's very hard to describe sex without making the partic-
ipants sound either like gods or dogs—whereas a fifty–
fifty combination of the two would be a lot more like it.

I am engaging in sexual intercourse with another person. This is happening. Should I really be doing this?
There is ivy against the window.

It is bouche more than it is Mund or mouth; it is Ruch
more than back or dos; it is sigh more than soupir or
Seufzer; it is equally l'amour and Liebe and love.

I know one is meant to think about irrelevances whilst
one is having intercourse, particularly when it is going
very well or very badly, but I find it hard to believe the
world exists beyond the realm of two skins in increas-
ingly sweaty contact.

One sometimes wishes it were less like ritual and more
like sport. For example, I—like many other men—feel
an agreed points system would be a boon.

Few things apart from sexual intercourse make one realize how physiological our existence is. As we become more and more liquid, we realize in quite how many ways we—day to day—flow.

It is hard to generalize about an experience so specifically diffuse.

There's a moment when their spine bends forwards over one and the blankets are around, of echoing inside the created cavern of the other; tidal, submersive.

Imagine the pressure—this fuck is eternal; get it wrong and it will never ever go right: one will fail for ever. The responsibility, though, wasn't mine-in-the-present-moment. It had all been decided so far in the past that I just relaxed and let what was anyway going to happen happen.

Gamblers don't like sex because it's much too much like gambling.

At moments you are known to have implanted I still don't know how to finish this sentence . . .

One feels as if, in finding oneself, one has also been most delightfully found out.

We turn blind corners, during, and emerge completely unpredictably onto triumphant dead-ends or bump bewildered into endless vistas of gorgeousness.

The harder she clasps you, the deeper you are into enemy territory; after.

Then one begins to feel like a dancer turning into a classical sculpture, and wishing one were a better dancer so as to make a more graceful shape for the marble.

Enswathed in such a soul, how could one not become more and more Russian? Wispy whispers in a whirly world.

Beauty is straitened youth; Beauty is straightened Youth.

Small hairs sprouting from all the vowels except *i*.

When we exchanged souls, I was not confused; in the giving-away, both gained.

Winkingly: I never knew a thing like it, apart from all the other things like it that I never knew.

Being a witch being a witch being me being a witch.

At this point, I begin to feel like a yeti under an eggnog waterfall; she—I know—begins to feel like a seamonster in a volcano.

As we couple, he thinks about money, which has ceased to exist, or ceased to have currency, and he is overwhelmingly relieved, and comes.

This is a disaster; I am thinking.

Of all things here, apart from suicide, money is the most trivial.

The Prodigal Son: penetration equals homecoming; ejaculation equals forgiveness; breathing equals breathing.

We lay, our legs swastikaed across each other, as if both taking a giant step forwards.

The wood sounded for a moment as if it had been listening to us, as if this were the only thing we might do that might make it listen.

As always, the cup and saucer on the chair.—"Could you pass it to me, please?"

The fetched water tasted of green, long.

Her stomach has its own music.

I never have any idea how long this lasts.

The blankets which once sang like an organ.

"Come outside," says Olwyn. "This is the time it rains."

I thought—I did at least think—not "How is she so certain it's about to rain?" but "Why is she saying it's about to rain in this particular way?"

We were both naked. "Don't worry," Olwyn said, "No-one comes." I told her I'd already climbed the tallest tree in The Darkenings, naked. "I know," she said.

The scent of raindrops starting to fall onto the arched tortoiseshell back of midsummer.

For a little while—before the dark mud forms—dust marbles over the surfaces of waterglobes, and droplets pattern their distribution on mushroom outposts.

One waits to see which way it will go—increased humidity or staying puddles?—this English foretaste of how a rainy season might begin.

Rain on skin; rain between skins.

We could be rivers, they seem finally to say. We will be puddles!

After dancing like wild things, we sauntered back into the hut.

Straggle hair on snuggle head.

Noon-sleep: This was a summer when England was lionized, visually.

Like a proper animal, one disposed-disported oneself in relation to the heat; radiant testicles.

In an attempt to feel cooler than I was, I fabricated an entirely imaginary breeze.

Incandescence; There is no higher height, there is no faster fall—simultaneously.

Rippled out with blowy orchard-light.

To the far edge of The Darkenings, clothed, together— because Olwyn leads me, for something to be seen.

The light on the flanks of a galloping horse; your beauty, Olwyn.

I have to ask the question, "How did I get here?" I mean, to begin with; not the aeroplane, Jens and Jurgen.

One sees himself walking through a horse; through and out.

It was a horse or a vision of a horse or a dream of what a vision of a horse might be, and in my devastated state it no longer really mattered which—I was just as likely, just as unlikely, to ride a vision as I was to ride a horse.

You wished you had been able to see it better, to see it as George Stubbs (1724–1806) or Eadweard Muybridge (1830–1904) or a Leica III might have seen it.

The failure of the human, that is, the failure that makes the human human, is the failure to recognize oneself as as inescapable to one's being as horse is to horse.

He wished to be able to act with himself—he had always wished not to be soul-divorced into considerer and considered. If he had not torn his souls apart, he would have torn himself apart. And all this from within the unthinking canter of a mare, probably to escape the annoyance of a gadfly.

"No, I wouldn't make you into one, even if I could," Olwyn says. "New horses are always noticed."

At moments you are happier than you feel yourself capable of being.

I was between the trees.

One sees himself walking through a house.

I have to ask the question, "How do you transport a
human soul?" I mean, without a body.

Tiny writing. Scrambled eggs are a dish one should
make only for oneself, and eat standing up, or for a love
with whom one has—within the hour—copulated. No
restaurant in the world is able to serve them properly;
the distance between hob and plate is too great. The
eggs go beyond their optimum; to cook them at the
table, before the diner, is swank; this is a domestic dish.
Here is my recipe. Put the tomatoes on under the grill
eleven minutes before you wish to eat, they must be
blackened. Ready a china bowl, either three or six fine
not-fresh eggs, the other ingredients as well. Place a
small saucepan on a medium heat, then drop in enough
butter to cover the base. Into the china bowl break the
eggs, add a whiff of white pepper, a fingernail of
mustard powder and a fingerbob of cream of the milk.
Whisk, but only with a fork and not as if you really
meant to whisk. Add two pinches of salt, one from
either hand. Pour the egg-mixture into the pan and
whatever you do don't fuss with it. Stir enough to keep
it from omeletting on the base, no more. Do not stir
constantly. The tomatoes should be almost ready. Are
you having toast? Factor this in for yourself. If the flame
looks likely to cook the egg in three minutes, turn it
down. Cook until the mixture has ceased to be a liquid
but is still pourable. The scrambled egg must scramble
sideways when poured, not drip, not roll. The plate on
which they land should be white and warm. At this
point, you should be able to smell the idea of chickens

in the kitchen. Cutlery should be ready to hand, so there is no delay in getting to the eating. If possible, burn the top of your mouth slightly with the first mouthful. That is all.

At moments you are happier than you feel yourself capable of ever having been.

"That is my favourite meal," says Olwyn. "Thank you."

Olwyn asked me what I could remember of the time before the camp.

> At first I can remember very little of the time before the camp.

Only stones own their own lives.

I suppose I thought it strange that Olwyn suddenly took an interest in my past; although, at the time, I seem to have just accepted it as a consequence—a natural following—of what we had just done. The conversation had begun when our mouths met; speaking in tongues. But she had never shown any curiosity about who I was or the life I had led. It had always seemed as if she already knew when I was likely to say what I was going to say. And, in a way, this had given me another excuse not to think about it myself. Because I didn't want to think about it. Because it was painful to think about. Because it was so vague—parts of it, anyway.

> At first I almost begin to suspect that the time before the camp did not exist.

You have a house. You have a father. You have a knife.

For this, I am sitting in the Windsor chair and Olwyn is lying in the bed. Her left breast is exposed, with the hard pink-brown puckering of the aureole and a few snail-trails running sideways. Her hair is what I and the rain have made of it. One of her eyes is on me, the other looks elsewhere. I feel I could tell this woman anything, and she would already have forgiven me for it.

> Then, when I do remember, the experience is so extreme that I cannot say it, and I do not know how I have forgotten it.

> They arrived but not in a boy's wishful drawing of a spaceship.

I got back in bed, to delay the talking.

> They were definitely they. There were no lights in the sky because there was no sky.

> Impossible forms: They were so other, and the senses by which they impressed themselves upon me were prosthetic, temporary; this language I have just will not do.

We fun and joy upon the morning.

> One might report it all through vaguenesses—bright lights, tingling sensations, sleep-wake cycles; and most of it is vague, conceptually if not physically.

> They arrived in a boy's wishful drawing of a spaceship.

> There were no lights in the sky because there was no sky.

When I stood face-to-face with one of the blighters, I realized he didn't have a face.

And an interlude of intertwining. And an afternoon of swoon.

They took me by force. I thought they were putting me into the back of a van, but it can't have been.

I went down into a thick golden liquid that I remember as being full of rising bubbles but I know this is false; my lungs were taken over by the liquid, emptied of oxygen. One didn't need to breathe, which was a horrible sensation. What if one suddenly returned to an oxygen-world? Would one have forgotten how to breathe? Would one's chest muscles have atrophied hopelessly? Would one drown in syrup?

I have the feeling of staying more still than I have ever done before, no world whirling beneath me. Then I am elsewhere, and the speed of light hasn't even been invoked.

What I wanted was a view, yet I understood it was a condition of this golden travelling place that no-one could merely look outside it. To go somewhere else so fast, the voyage would be held up by tendrils of clinging light, seen. Yet if the place didn't quite know where it was, it would be there before it mattered.

There were no lights in the sky because there was no sky.

One became of the same substance as the place. Yet as I understood it, this granted only longevity, not immortality. Component liquids were perishable.

There was no terror of loss of identity; ladle out any equivalent amount of liquid and it would have been pure me. (This liquidity should have prepared me for being a rat. But it was the rest of my life which had failed to do that.)

Inside, one could move around as freely as if one were in the open air; the closer one got to the peripheries, the greater the resistance one met—slow me down so I don't fall out into emptiness.

If one ran at the wall of it, one bounced off. The best technique was to lead with one's fingers, as if one were a Victorian stage ghost feeling its way—through muslin—in to disturb the next scene.

Bless with bliss the glad and good.

Everything distorted, and the place as a whole smeared across the emptiness. We were like dough beneath a rolling-pin, surging towards a flatness we never reached.

For the briefest of whiles we did not know where we should be going, and then we found we had arrived where we had all along wanted to be.

A scene for a conversation was constructed in my head. Information could merely have been given to me— instructions—but they wanted me to have the illusion of agency.

If they had had hands, I would have shaken them.

A conversation was imagined, within the flow, and I was party to it. My life was described to me, the logic behind it. I followed, could see no reason for objecting to listening.

There was another long journey followed by a short rest followed by a long journey followed by the word follow.

The golden liquid evaporated; my lungs worked; one wished it had felt less like waking from a nightmare.

What I remember after this is: I was in a white place, for quite some time.

There were cells which were colder than bracken or windowpanes.

There were rooms I wasn't allowed to leave before I had forgotten almost entirely that anything outside the room existed.

There were pylons, curtseying and curtseying, as we drove along beside them.

There was heart-breaking kindness from people one knew one would never meet again, because the kind people always disappeared, that was the rule.

There were invasions of the body and disturbances of the mind.

There was an inability to trust; there was no-one worthy of one's trust.

There was deception followed by mockery, there were confidences followed by shame.

There was water that tasted of iron and sugar that tasted of salt.

There was welcoming the sharp new pain because it stopped one feeling the aches of the old pains.

There were places where years of lifetimes, one could feel, had been wasted.

There was a hatefully inefficient bureaucracy.

There were mysterious overnight departures of which one was never given advance warning.

There was a bureaucracy of distilled contempt.

There were threats which were issued and never carried out, although they had poisoned one's life for days.

There was sleep which had to be a state of alertness and wakefulness that was only maintained at the price of trance.

There was, once, marmalade—home-made marmalade. Mostly, there were cornflakes. Cornflakes heaped high and piled higher still with sugar. But the marmalade, confusingly, didn't come from one of the kind people. A total bastard had made the delicious marmalade.

There were interludes beyond this.

There was an end, which was around about when Germany invaded Poland and the Second World War began.

It became impossible to tell whether my father was my grandfather or not, so I invented my grandfather. A mess.

I told all this to Olwyn, who listened as if she were
hearing a familiar song. She almost hummed along,
when I came to the gold and before that the marmalade.

I seem to be exhausted, in more than a normal way, and
I fall into a fairytale sleep.

Remember, we are still living in the midst of a silent
rookery; it cloaks us—as much to prevent me escaping
as to protect the house from spies or invaders. There are
rook-presences in my dreams.

A hill never feels steeper than when one has to run up it,
pursuing or pursued.

I go into a kind of late Autumn of the soul, perhaps
because it is so many-leaved.

Even to yourself you pretend you have become accus-
tomed to the close company of a thousand rooks,
although you sense they enjoy spying on you. The only
time they take off is when the London train goes past.
Strangely, when it heads North, the same engine, they
do not rattle a wing.

Outside in the Lloyd Loom chair: There was a lilt to
the lift of the air of the day; it had time, so it seemed,
for a dallying line from hither to yon, from surface to
stratosphere.

Does one really have to convalesce after telling a story?

It was flowing, the world—the around-me-immediately,
what for so long had been concrete or at best porridge
was now glister-water. The sight of it made me change

allegiance: I will not kill anyone grown from this land—
not even my grandfather's father. But then I realize
| that I am already a traitor beyond redemption. What I
want is the land without my language—the land where
mother-tongue is replaced by muttersprache, and house
by Haus, landscape by Landschaft, air by Luft, head by
Kopf, tree by Baum, river by Fluss, child by Kind, moon
by Mond.

Since I have stopped talking to her, Olwyn has become
much better disposed towards me; one might even say
that she's taken a shine. Because I am suddenly so little
bother, Olwyn begins to make me cups of tea.

I let my head sink to my breast.

It seems the more truly disinterested one is, the
more seductive one becomes; of course, this is unfair
to lovelorn souls, and unfair in a different way to
psychopaths.

She begins to half-sing to herself because she knows I
am only half-listening to her.

Rooks never became a mere ambience—it was as if one
were living in a castle where the inner walls were lined
with steel spikes.

Enjoy these moments, my solitary reader, then make
sure you go and catch the last of the sunlight before it
leaves the doorstep.

The rooks make not only the trees and the whole wood
but even the sun itself feel more ancient.

(I think this is the most one can do in life, enjoy the being in the light—however difficult and debateable the being of that being is.)

Birdsong is off-puttingly beautiful.

The cats sometimes follow me out to watch me urinate; they are most fascinated when it is sunny.

Conversation with Olwyn; quote.

All I had to do was stop doing things, it seems, and I became acceptable—both to Olwyn and to myself.

This is not a conversation we had; these words were not passed between us, in this order, but this is exactly what we said to each other (over the course of about a week):

"You are not as clever as you like to think," she says, and I reply, "I don't think I'm clever at all."

"The way you speak and the way you treat me—" And I say, "I wasn't brought up to be ill-mannered."

"But you were brought up to be heartless." "I am full of respect for you."

"I think you don't know what the heart is used for." "What would you have me do? I don't understand. When I do nothing, you accuse me of laziness. When I try to help, you reject it—you rebuff me."

"Whoever rebuffed anything? I told you you were doing it all wrong, that's all." "Isn't that telling me not to do it?"

"You need to have some human feelings, that's what I mean—you need to realize, despite what you've seen or say you've seen, that we're all in this mess together." "And what should we do?"

"Do things right or not do them at all." "You don't talk like this."

"I don't talk like anything—what comes out of my mouth comes out, I never think anything particular of it." "But what do you think?"

"My time is different from yours—my time is worse."

A gentleman should take domestic politics slightly less seriously than backgammon.

The moon is my only month.

I don't believe we are good, because of what we want to do; any monster can be well-intentioned.

Calendar-hoax: "My time is different from yours—my time is harder."

All of a sudden does not always happen all of a sudden.

A period of time is over; the fat moon is thinning.

I miss the rainfall tickle of words inside my eyeballs; the slow cool seepage of them back into the brain.

That Olwyn can be located at a certain map-reference, that she displaces a certain volume of air, that she pertains at all to the world of facts—impossible!

I am tracking Olwyn's memories, as I would track a wounded deer. One intends very much to bring it down.

I missed the shapes of the letters formed into the and and and but.

"Tell me what you remember of your childhood," I say. And Olwyn tells me, and it is marvellous, but it is hers, hers to keep. I will steal one thing only—she watched a sparrow die.

All I want is a book to fit in the hand with some words in.

It wasn't like I was asking for flamboyance or rococo or opulence or filigree.

I am thinking of my grandfather's library—a place for sitting and smoking and talking. A place for killing.

All of a sudden, I had felt the need to read something.

All those books, pressed shut; pages not opened since they were printed in 1821 or 1605. I wanted them to moth, to fly towards my itch eyes.

"Do you have any books?" I asked Olwyn.

"Why would I need a book?" she said, shaking her head like an old blind woman.

The thought of frontispieces, titles, black letters—there would be a few words in the card-index; perhaps some overdone eighteenth-century titles that would take me more than a second to read.

All of a sudden, I realized I did have something to read.

"The Most Marvellous and Unprecedented Adventures
of Osbert Ostrich-Allen, Esquire, Gentleman, in the
Divers Lands and Empires of the New New Worlds, by
His Good Friend and Companion William Smidgeon,
Surgeon."

In the camp I had borrowed books. For the mission,
they had not allowed me to carry anything with writing
on. My story was that I was illiterate. You have no
papers. I have no papers.

> Card-index: Olwyn has gone down to the well, to fetch
> the day's bucket. I wanted to go down with her, but she
> wouldn't let me. "It's not safe," she said. "You need to
> stay here for now."

Jens and Jurgen told me my story, but how could they
have known the end? Boys, are you dead yet? I hope you
have more than tasks in your wartime—some lovely
correspondent, not necessarily the blondest, but probably, knowing you. (Handsome ones.) And you smell the
paper as it rises from the envelope, for a moment,
flowers—you dance around the village square as grandmothers smile; you knew the best shadows whereto
escape from those watchers with brown teeth and
embarrassing familiar knowledge. This kiss is in no way
the same as the shadow-kiss of your father and mother,
years ago. You inhabit, both and both, the modern
touch. The world will be better for these clean tres-
passes; Aryan. A simplicity of fabric meets a complexity
of fabric, button-caught. Jens did not confess this;
Jurgen failed to let on.

All idylls have always seemed as unreal to me as
Tennyson's of the King; even ones I myself have
experienced.

    The handwriting on the cards of the card-index was
    neat, male, unfamiliar; the handwriting on the front of
    the cards, that is.

    I flicked through one index after another, forwards and
    back—it was like being inside a computer; it was like
    being a computer.

The moment one thinks one's happiness complete,
one's happiness ends.

    Olwyn seems not to be returning, through the curtain
    of rooks. She has left me to this; she has left this to me.
    Time to sit down.

    How ignorant am I really of what I am about to
    discover?

Someone will enjoy this.

    I climbed onto the card-index—it was quite strong
    enough to take my weight—and sat there for a moment
    before opening the first drawer.

    Because of where I was sitting, because of picking up
    the cards from that position, I approached them in a dif-
    ferent way; backwards.

    I see that there is something on the back of each card,
    dark horizontal lines, broken, tiny when it needs to be.

Imagine my shock—witness my shock—as I picked out the first of the cards and saw, upon the back, my own handwriting. How did I know it was my own hand-writing, when I had written nothing that I could remember? Because I did, the moment I saw this |sen-tence, remember writing it.

Who-am-I? Why-am-I-here? Where-am-I-going? Why-am-I-going-there? Ghost-questions; fast.

The handwriting on the back of the card, in pen and pencil, with rubbings out and writings over read:

"You do not begin reading at the beginning. You begin at the top of this card, with this line; you read this sen-tence, and the sentence following, and then obediently read the next card before going back to the first card. That's what you do, believe me."

The next card read: "After this, you will turn back to the first card. Because before you make any decisions you must read all of this. It has been prepared for you, by you, more painstakingly than either of us can imagine. Be grateful; feel satisfied. There is no rush, although you hurry." I read the card after it, which I was not meant to read, although I was.

I shuffled along the index, almost to the far end, pulled out another card from another drawer, and this one read:

"Olwyn will say, 'I have been waiting for extinction—impatiently, I'm afraid.'"

Quickly, I checked another card, then another, then another. Upon all of them I—my handwriting—seemed to have written something. How? In my sleep? In a previous visit here? But I had not been here before, had I?

Off the card-index, leaving drawers open—I must find Olwyn—Landing hard on my ankle but not injuring it—The cup and saucer on the table—Out the door—The blankets on the bed—Never mind if I am seen—Never mind if Gaiters catches me—Out, into the clearing—I am confused—I am my own explanation—I have to know—The rooks explode from the boughs—Olwyn knows—Olwyn will hear the rooks—The cup and saucer on the table—Everyone will hear the rooks—

A gentleman is at home everywhere, but has only one true home—the field of battle.

I rush through panic that takes the form of trees with low hanging branches. But running to Olwyn, I run straight into Olwyn.

My only month is the moon.

"I will explain," Olwyn says, before I even get the chance to ask her what in hell's name is going on.

If I knew myself, I would know what question I would want to ask.

"You have been here before," she said. "You have been here countless times, but each time you go away and you forget."

Some of one's most vivid experiences take place in the future tense.

"But—" I said.

"You will understand, if you go and read what you have written before. Oh, I can't be bothered with this," she hits me on the chest. "Go. I've lost you to it now."

"But—" I will say.

"It is very hard on me," said Olwyn. "It is annoying, but at least I get some respite—and I get to torture you for a while. In your ignorance. You've always insisted upon that."

To insist upon one's similarity to other men is to exhibit one's Messiah complex.

"And now," she said, "you will go back to the card-index."

And now it feels as if someone has just cracked an egg, an ordinary egg, into my heart: the shell isn't in this—I'm not talking about anything as simple as a broken heart; it's more—it's more—that I can feel the soft flow of something alien, cooling, part-transparent, part-gaudy, within my body's shivered core. Subject.

I go back to the card-index with the fear of love of death of love in me: there are secrets here, not just other men's. It reeks of them, the long box, and of the finger-tips of the curious. I look at the length of it. I will sit and read; herd.

A gentleman should never keep a diary—to pay attention to one's own affairs suggests one may wish to profit thereby.

Oh, look at this ink, flowing in curlicues across the
page—and the words all a-scrabbling to keep up!

Transition from alarm to fascination, through reading;
ten minutes.

One finds one makes discoveries as exultantly as if one
had also discovered discovery itself. Starting top left.

Swimming through tadpoles. You really feel as if you
have found something, don't you?

After a while I began to find it a little uncomfortable, up
on the card-index, so I jumped down and fetched myself
some pillows and a cup of tea.

Position-shifting-confusion: With an open drawer
between my dangling legs, it was easy to flick through
the notes—for that is what these turned out to be.

I am quite high up, sitting cross-legged here; the cats
join me, knock over my tea; I find I don't mind.

Where I was, I was comfortable; I knew I had been in
this position before, multiple times—this was the process for bringing the notes into being. If I hadn't
enjoyed the process, enjoyed it enough to tolerate it,
there would have been no product. Each card-index card
had one or more lines of script across the top, in my
handwriting, in my handwritings—I varied a great deal
from note to note; sometimes I angled forwards into a
possible future, sometimes I was upright with feigned
respectability and sometimes I was near-illegible with
the time-shame of it all. If ever I became completely
incomprehensible, another pencil-me would come

along patiently beneath to try to guess out the anger or sloppiness. But when I turned the cards around, I saw that their alphabetical order had been disrupted—misfires, incoherences, first-draft self-singing had been removed. I found them, the discards, in the lower drawers, scribbled and re-scribbled—and there were many more of them than was good for the maintenance of one's sanity.

You fetch pen, pencil. The room smells suddenly of walnuts. This, although I do not know it, is the beginning of a happy time, the writer-time, almost as happy as the rat-time.

You will know that what you have always suspected is true—that you are familiar with this world.

When I find a note that's wrong, I change it or replace it or move it to make it right in that place.

This is not a paperback.

I felt as if the drawers were opening themselves, the cards were fluttering in winglike pairs up to my eyes, and the words were being rewritten even as I read them. Their motion, rising, was not smooth; it seemed they flickered through quanta.

I am human; you are human: a tiny string, of course invisible, emerges from each pore of my body and makes its way into each pore of your body—this is our understanding, to do this. You are reading because my strings have twizzled all through you and climbed up behind your eyes. Yet the eyes with which I saw my words forming had already been invaded by your winking filaments. Each string, civilization.

I feel, as so rarely in life, that I have in one moment found and been found.

Some notes extended over two, three or more cards; some were just a pencilled word.

Sing, you over there!

Olwyn comes in after I've been like this for a couple of hours and says, "Now that looks familiar . . . "

I will have made entirely new re-discoveries.

That one is in inescapable time, or something like that. It is hard.

The card-index had originally been alphabetical, by author, and some few vestiges of this remained—every fourth or fifth card, reversed, was in the right relation to the one immediately after, but my constant shuffling had disordered the whole device.

I want to explain it to her, but she has absolutely no use for that.

"Watch this," said Olwyn.

Olwyn walks outside to catch—without looking—a yellow leaf as it falls from a tree; she knows the world this better than well.

Olwyn says, "If we wait here for another five minutes, the fox will come past—over there, just behind that bush."

And we wait, and the fox comes.

"In the High Field, a shotgun fires at just after ten o'clock."

We listen to the church bells; we listen to the report.

Witch.

"This is how I know when to bury you," says Olwyn. "Because they come looking, then. Otherwise, you get caught and have to escape to finish it."

It is easier now to understand Olwyn's manner, her atrocious balancing act. She does not look a day younger, but I see her as something quite refreshed.

"If I don't stop you, you will try to kiss me. My time is different to yours."

Now I begin to understand the rain.

It is written here that I love Olwyn in a way I had not recognized until I read it written here.

If I smell my own fingers, they show me a thousand years of graphite; tree-shaped.

Everything initially happens eternally.

How is it possible to walk wisely? And yet she does— and yet she does; even from her tread, one can tell she knows more about Life than one will ever learn.

"What do I do now?" I ask Olwyn, who has already taken me by the hand and started to lead me towards the hut. She leads me up to the card-index. "You ignore me," she says.

It is not weariness yet it is not sparkle; it is pure response.

The task invents the tool.

Not the knife, the soul.

This must have been how I worked—pulling out a handful, then flicking through them one after another, making changes.

Impatience is the desire to make time flow backwards. And even writing the word makes me laugh—Flow!

This—are you listening?—was the sound of writing, was for a few thousand years: the fabulous, scrabulous traverse, the scrunch-line of thin nib (wood, bone, quill, metal) meeting paper and leaving sense. Yes, scrunch—the downstrokes are the most definite; the vowels sound like self-mutterings. When a comma comes, or a full-stop, it's not quite as momentous as a raindrop on the back of your hand. The most elegant sounds are the flourishing swirls of *g* and *f* and *q* and *y*—a little grouch followed by a quiet yawn. Then comes the din of ascenders and descenders—literally appalling flying latterly; how much more expression in that than in moon, woman, answers, crimson.

You are your own—don't include this—recording angel. This is your own earthbound Akashic record; discard.

This is your experience—this is the scope of your experience—all that is left is for you to work on your memory. If one day, you can get a message to yourself to experience things more minutely, that would be useful. As it is, we are relying on the memories of an insufficiently attentive man.

"I want you to be as little bother as possible," Olwyn says, over dinner. "I've tried it other ways—this is the best of them."

The amazing thing in these notes is, a devastated person who is—yet—prey to presence of mind; yet.

Wisdom is a map of everything but the timeless.

I thought to test; to test, I thought. So, I remembered, recalled.

A woods has appeared in the tent, evening into night.

The bonfire in The Darkenings is like someone using a star for kindling.

I fear someone is camping, lighting fires, impossibly intruding; they may even be female.

I go to spy upon them in human form; they are not interesting; I return—I feel I have done what I should.

"I told you so," said Olwyn.

Why are they not interesting? Because they are not Olwyn. They were younger than her, and had things moving in their hair. One of them had teeth that pointed slightly inwards, which made me think she was a good rat. The other sang, badly.

I would say they are gypsies, though that would mean there should be men.

The following night, this bright particular star does not come out.

This counts as an episode.

What are your earliest memories? **Answer.**

"I don't know," Olwyn answers, in the dark. "I had the whole thing brought from the library, when they left it out in the rain. The librarian was a visitor of mine. He was crying, but had no choice. I can't read. I thought I could burn it."

Sleepless: One can't corrupt one's entire sensibility, but one can't keep it out of harm's way either: a sensibility is a distinctive choice of harms.

Everything in and of the hut does not merely smell of woodsmoke, it is as if everything were fashioned of solidified **woodsmoke. Especially Olwyn.**

What we must keep is not our Humanity but our Energy.

I am trying to recall the memories that do not feel as though they should belong to me.

I sleep, and when I wake in the morning Olwyn has taken away my suit.

The first syllable of scissors has turned into something else—silken black, elegant, grotesque.

Of course, I have many memories, but I cannot think of them without discovering the person to whom they do not belong.

"Why do I have to wear a dress?"

"It will keep you safe," she says. "I made it for you."

I feel I have absolutely no right to these memories; my inexistent identical twin is coming to reclaim them: and it is gladly I will give them up.

I can recall things I know I should not be able to recall because whilst they were taking place I was off else-where, waiting to be born.

"It will hide you," she said. "When the time comes for you to be hidden."

I recall an always garden mother because

I recall a dead bird in the car park, a sparrow chick, with eyes that bulged like two slit testicles on the left side of its twistedness, and the smell coming from the dead fallen-from-the-nest chick on the unsmooth grey Tarmac was of boiling treacle.

I put on the black dress, which has been made to fit me.

I recall the smell of grass scythed; smell not scent; scythed not mown.

I recall my mother in the twilight in the twilight of my mother; I recall the grey from outside overtaking first the room, then her.

Of some things ink is unworthy and paper does not merit the confidence. This is not my present opinion.

I recall arriving home just in time to see my grandfather hurrying off in the opposite direction.

I must say I have been bewitched.

I recall the solid moth fluttering into my mother's face and, as he bashed it to death, the confused hate buried within the face of my grandfather. Was it for moth or mother?

I recall so little, few events, only differently savoured spaces. I recall spending a lot of time looking at the ground; War-clouds.

I recall the the school playground, no area so dense with significance before or since.

I recall walking across an open concrete quadrangle, though I do not recall where I was walking to or from, or why I was there, or what the place was—if I try, though, I can still feel that particular air-box around me.

I recall looking through the windscreen at the three lanes of the motorway and thinking one could as well lie down and sleep on them as drive down them at eighty-five miles an hour.

I recall walking along the edge of a wide, dew-damp field as the evening light varnished the copper corn.

I recall the warm concrete of 1976—it was quite different to the warm concrete of either the preceding or the
subsequent years.

I recall an open field beneath a row of pylons, those
overhead wires with their perpetual x'xxx'xx, and the
grass cropped short by either cows or sheep. I lay there
until I got bored, which cannot have taken long; I was a
panicker.

I recall very distinctly it being 1974, although I cannot
recall a thing that happened that year.

> In my dress, I search for my suit, and of course I can't
> find it.

I recall advertising slogans but not the voices that sold
them.

I recall many episodes of birdsong, intermittently,
undedicated, throughout my life—and these, it turns
out, have been more enduring than any conversation.

I recall being driven up to and past an avenue of trees—
how the two long lines of uprights pulsed with patterns
before, for one clear moment, snapping into perspective
on a house, and then reversing their patterned pulse
almost exactly.

I recall the hawk, hovering beside the motorway, which
did not dive before we were out of sight, if it ever did.

I recall the closer, larger trees sliding in front of the slow
middle-distance ones behind a whizzing screen of green
leaves held by branches anchored to trunks that—seen
distantly—hardly seem to move at all.

I recall tall glasses of perfect milk, drunk too fast—
always drunk too fast.

I recall the electricity substation on the edge of a sheep-
field where I would climb the brick wall and look over
across the backs of the sheep towards something I can't
recall.

I recall, again, acres of transfixing, overlapping
boredoms.

I recall so very clearly the honesty I never felt I had;
moments of indecision; its contours so clear I might
have made a sculpture out of it; majestic and heroic.

I recall differently bleak-blank areas of waiting time, that
I had that I had to cross over over and over if ever I was
going to be able to live in hope of an actual over event.

I recall realizing that I would never be as good at being
one specific person as the person I wanted to be would
have been.

I recall when a phone might ring for half an hour, or
half a day, because it was very important that it was
answered, whenever it might be answered.

I recall the denied elation around deaths; the lace anti-
macassars were to be vanquished, one by one.

I recall climbing trees and falling out of trees.

I recall my room is my grandfather's room; I recall my
room as my grandfather's room.

One recalls the physical sensation of falling, as if it had lasted for hours and days.

I recall reading certain books and I am sure that I read more books than I can recall reading.

One recalls no instances of transcendent light—this is a lie: truthfully, one recalls almost nothing but.

I recall the shower of sparks rising from the bonfire of peat; aetherial.

I recall the light-through-honey of the final day of school before the summer holidays.

I recall finding great significance in particular cloud-moments in particular skies, though I cannot recall where I was when I observed them—though I some-times think I can recall the feel of the clothes I was wearing, soft or itchy at the cuffs and seams.

People, it seems, I cannot recall. The cut-out shapes of where they used to be are still there, sort of. But they are like the figures walking through architectural mod-els, white, pointing and anonymous. We don't care any more about them, although we know that we should feel that we should.

I recall there are people who are famous but their importance now eludes me, and I cannot connect one to the other. A few of them must have been associated with music and fast movement. And there were some games with balls, weren't there? And it was very impor-tant to some people who won and who lost, although many people also took almost no notice.

One recalls her perfume, like bonfires burning to the left and right of one. Her? Which her?

I recall the cars in traffic jams but not the drivers or passengers of those cars, neither do I remember their makes.

One recalls the waiting rooms—the many waiting rooms—far better than the appointments.

One recalls music, and one recalls where one was when one heard it, but one does not recall if it was played by an orchestra or on the radio.

One recalls Mozart and Schubert, Wagner and Bach— who are not all German.

I recall the moth in the twilight, and the bright face.

I recall the golden liquid, and now I have caught up with myself. The gold.

I recall no-one apart from Hitler, Churchill, my grandfather, Gaiters and this sentence is already too long.

I do not recall a time when I did not have this hangnail on my right thumb.

And thus I am convinced—I do not recall the time I should have lived through; I am anachronism. Yet nowhere in the card-index does it say what happens after a planned attempt to kill Churchill, myself wearing a black silk dress. This comes fairly soon.

And so what does one conclude? One concludes that these memories are structural rather than real; steel struts to fill out the chickenwire rocks of my mind. My start-point is closer to this moment than birth.

I felt very melancholy when I thought of all the friends I must once have had, yet had now forgotten.

So appalled by one's youth that one finds oneself incapable of experiencing it—except as the state of being appalled.

Am I such a fool as to never have been capable of doing anything other than the foolish things I have done? If someone had been able to say to me, earlier on, what was to happen, surely I could have prevented myself? No? Not at all? Have I merely fulfilled someone else's potential?

A great deal of shuffling has gone on—shuffling seems to be my modus operandi; grab a handful of cards, read the cards through, shuffle them, read the cards through, shuffle them, et cetera . . . (This hut is an et cetera at the moment.)

Olwyn continues to make me cups of tea; I continue not to speak.

It does give me, the shuffling, something in which and from which to take respite, refuge.

Of course, I have memories, but I cannot think of them without discovering the person to whom they do not belong.

This world comprehensively is too full of worlds desperately for one person abstractly to dwell in it beautifully.

I find I have absolutely no right to these memories; my inexistent identical twin is coming to reclaim them: and it is gladly I will give them up.

A gentleman should enter the room as if he has never existed before, and depart in the manner of an eternal verity.

My childhood did not just belong to another person, that other person had another childhood that didn't belong to them.

I have come across a note saying how I have now mapped the card-index. Top left to bottom left, there is a continuous run of cards, telling the story from the beginning, beginning with "It was spooked England"; most of the other drawers contain drafts, roughest in the bottom drawer, best in the top; far right at the bottom, there is one drawer with the cards all missing.

If there were a second way to be myself, I am sure I would have discovered it.

A gentleman should, when facing any important decision, consult with his great-great-grandfather; Catcher.

Very few of the notes exist only in one form—many have been done and redone dozens of times. I find twenty-five versions of the sentence, "A gentleman— English—should reassure foreigners of his bona fides by appearing to be nothing more than a parody of an English gentleman; this is particularly important with Americans."

At least in my life I will have realized one thing, even if
that thing is that I will never realize more than that one
thing, over and over again.

This world is better made than if I had made it, of that I
am certain.

Zonk like a billiard ball socko-locko into the top pocket;
clat of the cue against the edge as the tipsy player stands
up and away from the table. How I yearn to be unnoticed in the corner of an English pub. I am a trick-shot.

Even the thought of endless repetition should have been
enough to drive one mad, and yet it hasn't already,
unless it already has.

What I miss most of all is the sea, although I suppose I
do get to see it through the bomb-doors.

Who knows what the first sentence you wrote was.

The moon is our only month.

The surfer and the soprano; their whelm-ripe realms—
whale-road and will-ride. Missed.

I have to see myself as comic; with such repetition,
there can hardly be heroism.

Unable: I can't explain how I can add to the notes but do
nothing else; Olwyn has repairs to the cottage which I
am never able to complete. (So you might as well not
bother, friend, unless it's just to show willing.) It's hard
to know when last I added anything of substance, here:
perhaps my previous time round, perhaps not for half

the length of the universe. I certainly don't feel like making any large changes. For many sentences, I am just a copyist; less than a reader; less than myself.

The qualities of these experiences were not diminished by their repetition, just as long as one lived in ignorance of one's true states; yet when the revelation occurred, one did not instantly become a state to oneself—the dulling took a day.

One does not believe he is lunatic.

The cats were now so constant a dual presence as to be near imperceptible.

If I succeed this coming time in killing my grandfather, surely I shall be released; hog-time.

I do not believe I have ever met Adolf Hitler or been on a spaceship or lain down in a cornfield or breathed in and out.

Conversations with Olwyn, in no particular order.

Youth, that already-fallen blossom. One feels one should remember everything else that is going to happen.

I was always reading about something that hadn't happened yet.

It is awful, only ever being with Olwyn. All this August—among bees and dandelions—I have hated the idea of speaking to anyone else.

The London train continues going to London.

Everything eternally happens initially.

When I consider my knife, it has become quite quite decorative.

The first things you wrote have long ago been replaced by something more apt.

I hung from the top of the tree, like a pair of binoculars.

It started as a game and became a form.

> "I know more about this war of yours than you think I do," said Olwyn.

I wish I could find a way to allow myself to rest. If I could rest more, I could work more. If I could work more, I would feel able to make a little more time available for resting. There are nubs and discolourations on the undersides of particular leaves I would like to spend some time examining. Not for gain. Not even for gain of knowledge or peace. Just because it, there, would be a good place for my eyes to find themselves, for a while, before I got them back to work.

Our feet always shuffled, as we moved around the camp; it was dangerous not to be heard to shuffle.

"I have been waiting for extinction—impatiently, I'm afraid."

The Führer is pushing me towards the coffin-shaped hole in the carpet.

> "Winston is coming down this weekend," she said.

I know all about the first attempt, having read about it.

When she rushes in through the door, the down-feathers of cat-killed sparrows waltz in her wake.

She says, "Winston will be in the library."

The badger will step on the rats as he runs from corner to corner of the remaining square; . . .

When she is in my arms, the feathers arrest their flight.

"Has Winston visited you?" Almost having not dared ask, but asking . . .

"Of course he has—he's a man, he's been near The Darkenings. I told you before, sooner or later they all come."

I am the cat who killed.

"What did he do?"

"Nothing unusual. Nothing the others didn't—not even the famous cigar. I've had that before. When they can't themselves."

One remembers men so agonized they began to miaow.

"How is he?" I asked. "As a man. As a person to be in a room with?"

"He makes a real effort to be rude but he can't help being polite. He's a gentleman. Not like you."

Olwyn says, "It is never September, you know."

Olwyn says, "I often wonder about September—what it must feel like. I am also curious about March."

Miaow.

A gentleman should never be heard to say anything other gentlemen have not said before.

Question: "Do I never discover the notes earlier? By myself?"

Answer: "Yes, but does that change a thing?"

Question: "Well, does it? I don't know. Does it?"

Answer: "You're here, aren't you?"

Question: "Am I here? How do I know I'm here? How do I know I'm not then or after instead? If I'm here, why aren't I better at being here?"

Answer: "You're still just a man. Men aren't much good at very much of anything—not so far as I can see."

Question: "But you must know more than that? Come on, Olwyn, you know more than you're letting on."

Answer: "What would you like to eat?"

Miaow.

Question: "Answer me—Why aren't I better at being here, if I've had so many rehearsals? Why can't I ask a better question than this?"

Answer: "I've never found asking questions got me anywhere."

Question: "Then what did?"

Answer: "Trying not to do anything, and then something happening anyway."

Question: "That helped? But that's just lazy."

Answer: "It's plenty too much work for some people."

Question: "Why aren't you amazingly wise? Why are you so commonplace?"

Answer: "I could ask you the same question, couldn't I?"

Question: "If one spends most of one's existence in complete ignorance of the true nature of that existence, then can one be anything other than un-wise?"

Answer: "That all sounds very well."

Question (Optional): "I sometimes think you're an imbecile, and that I'm trapped here with an imbecile, and that I will never get to talk to anyone but an imbecile."

Answer (Optional): "As if I care—as if any of this thrashing about makes any kind of difference—this scribbling. Don't you think we could spend the time much better?"

(I would I believe trade half my vocabulary to regain the lost eloquence of my cat-tail—)

Question: "Who are you, and what did we ever have to do with each other?"

Sadly: "I knew I should never take a man into my home—not even one who came accompanied by a hundred pure feet of black silk." Answer.

"When do you catch your last sight of me?"

"When do I catch my last sight of you?"

Some things, it doesn't matter who says them; some things are just said.

You are pretty sure that, previously, on many occasions, you have tried to escape the round.

"What if I just run away?"

The answer, my friend, is convoluted. In many of the pasts, you plural have tried to escape—we have attempted to steal or hijack cars and motorbikes; it has never come close to being successful. They have fled as fast as they could, heading out of Midfordshire, only to be caught. The furthest any of them has ever got is the main road—there is always someone waiting for us there, as elsewhere. We have begged Olwyn to return us to the form of the cat, and she has even given in, but the hounds found us. No method works, we can assure you. This system is closed. One can only suppose there is a meaning to this, albeit malign.

Accounts of your escapes may be found in the E section of the card-index, if you can be bothered to look there. I can't.

Next: Olwyn will tell you about what she said she was going to say about what happened before: How you had many times killed yourself.

"What about suicide? What if I jumped off the oak tree?"

"Kill yourself and you come back straight away."
Of all things here, apart from money, suicide is the most trivial.

And—to summarize—if you go to the house before Churchill is there, they will simply keep you prisoner until he has arrived, has contacted the War Room, has had dinner and has settled down in the library for a cigarette. In the end, the same basic events happen; you fail. Everything you are thinking of trying, you have tried before, believe us. After all this time, we are still ill-prepared.

"You can't keep away from that damned house, no more than blood can avoid the heart."

Answer: "I tried once telling you I loved you straight away—you thought it was a trap and strangled me."

Answer: "This is the way I make sure you come back."

"Turn me into a flying creature."

"You'll just have to be patient."

Olwyn: "My life has been over for longer than I can remember."

Myself: "There is nothing I would rather do than walk out of here and never return, apart from kiss you and stay for the rest of my life."

Myself: "Your total disregard for my feelings in this matter gives me great cause for concern." I despair.

"Then what can we do?"

"We can go for a walk," she says. "That is safe."

It is the evening.

For the first time, I am getting the sense that I know where things and people presently are and hence where they subsequently won't be (should I wish to avoid them); plot.

And now he starts to believe he can anticipate owl-hoots, wind-gusts, Olwyn's next yawn or stretch, tell every detail of occurrence. This is time-vanity, and worth you avoiding.

This is appalling, this absolute lack of uncertainty.

And one day, of this I assure you, it will end; I will end it; you will not have to read this again; you will not have to exist. All one needs to do is work out how to gain the strength.

The moon is their only month.

Instead, we go for a last walk together.

What kind of witch will I have been fashioning?

I recall no instances of transcendent light—this is a lie: truthfully, I recall almost nothing but.

Until this moment. Until these moments.

All it will take is for my knife once to do my thinking for me.

One less ivory greyhound—with no bottom jaw— among the walking-sticks. My grandfather's death.

The sky is pink on the horizon and blue at the zenith yet nowhere in-between is it a half-way colour.

I ask, "What happens to the silk? Where does it go?"

"I don't remember," she replied. "It comes with you. You're in my time, for me. I don't know about the future, and that's my future." I try to understand this just as she tries to say it.

Tiny gestures of helplessness . . .

The sharpened wooden stake of Autumn, abruptly entering Summer's chest cavity.

All assassinations are arachnoid.

"I have been waiting for extinction—impatiently, I'm afraid."

My chrome-and-neon nostalgia for the future.

What Olwyn tells me she misses most is Spring—that she is always seeing things at their height, but never at their new fresh weak birth.

Down evening comes over the visible plain, distressingly like nothing so much as a vast blue velvet curtain.

Until I became a cat, I thought I knew how cats like to be stroked.

My tongue travels up inside her, to become her teeth.

The rooks sounded as if they were minerals packing for a holiday.

It's not fair, he cried. I didn't want to weep. And then all of a sudden one found oneself in tears.

> Again when Olwyn goes for the water, I leave the house. This is the first new sentence in the book; the first sentence not in the card-index.

All this time, yes, still wearing the dress—quite used to it, by now.

Olwyn seems to believe that because she has memory of her past behaviours she therefore has free will.

The book. Perhaps a good idea not to mention the book yet.

I am happy that Olwyn's breath smells of me.

At the house they are busy with the harvest, and preparing for Winston's arrival.

I am confused I am not more happy.

It is hard to see how her psychology is constellated, or whether it can any longer be called a psychology.

Decline? And exactly which decline would that be?

When we have fought: Her radiant sympathy for anything and everything in the world—anything and everything but me.

> The card-index tells me this is the best time to go; this day.

When he woke, he found he had been lying so still that a spider had built its web over his left eye. Luckily, he realized this and was able to control his reflex before he had brushed it away. The spider was there, resting on his cheek, but the construction was too close for him to be able to focus on it. Enough.

I will miss this hut, for however long I am dead; I have come to need it.

Enough. This must end. One way or the other. This must end.

I decide to forget the whole Churchill shenanigan. All my knife wants is to kill my grandfather.

> If I understood the card-index properly.

My heart is signed, Hiroshima.

The orchard is behind the house; I do not get to the orchard.

I take my knife and leave the hut. The rooks make
noise, lots of noise; Olwyn will know. I want Olwyn to
know—but I am running towards The House Beautiful.
The silk dress feels exactly the wrong thing and exactly
the right thing to wear. You are not free.

"They come looking for you here again, tomorrow,"
says Olwyn.

There may yet be hope, although there seems to be
none.

My grandfather will be in the breakfast room.

My grandfather will be alone.

We are about to re-enter a more conventional brand of
time.

The house seems quiet; the house befits the morning; I
will not take risks—I will crawl through the wheat,
slowly, taking my time, taking half the morning.

A woman appeared, through the gate, dressed in blue
overalls—a maid I think I recognize. She stands, I wait;
she goes, I wait; I move. A dark shape.

It has been enjoyable, I must say, living in our future—
living in our future words.

Oh, you fool, you should have paid more attention to
the wheat earing up, listened to the rattle of the grain in
the husk!

A tractor engine will be heard.

You are right in the middle of the cornfield, very close to the pylon.

I should have known this was the day—the wheat looked on the point of turning pure lion's mane, still a while off blackening.

We are about to run out of fore-knowledge.

Here they come; to harvest the corn.

Of course, I try to retreat, but they are arriving from all directions—as they do.

I know what is going to happen, now—not from the card-index, which contains no mention that I have read, but because I have taken part in this ritual so many times before.

Blood, non-human blood, in small quantities is such a cheering sight. A little bit of Christmas, but always available.

My only advantage was to know the way the harvest always progressed. From an early age, I had been present—I must have been, for I remembered how they reduced the field to a small square of fluttering animal hysteria, then sent in the men with scythes. Not to allow anything to escape, they went at it from every direction at once.

The combine harvester would cut the wheat in from the edges, the baler coming behind; smaller and smaller would be the tall wheatstalks uncut—fuller and fuller of life.

Why do I feel it would be so much worse to die or be captured wearing a black silk dress?

Clouds never lose their dignity.

I was soon surrounded—women, and a very few men, all around the edges of the field; armed.

This is the latest card in the card-index. We do not know what happens after we set out, this morning, impulsively, murderously, towards the house, in dress, with knife.

Because the wheat was surrounded almost exclusively by women, I knew the killing would at least have ritual significance.

They might find me and shoot me and find me and then how they would laugh, the men, killing me a thousand times over—how Gaiters would laugh.

There's always a festive feeling builds up whenever small animals are about to be killed—it's a ritual of the country-folk all around the world, not just in England. Even from inside the crop, I could sense the anticipation surrounding me.

The edges of the cornfield had already been shorn away. The square at the centre was beginning to reduce in size.

I could just stand up, surrender. They would not shoot me, would they? Perhaps a woman.

Perhaps there was still a chance. Why had the card-index not mentioned this? Not only because it didn't go this far forwards in time. I am being prevented from knowing something, I think.

I heard my grandfather arrive; there were cheers of welcome from the land girls. My grandfather has come for the blood.

My grandfather overlooking the field from horseback sees me—I am sure he sees me; a black shape: target practice.

We walk through our blood; towards our blood.

The harvest continues, moment by moment, eyeblink by eyeblink, all morning—and I mention the sun, climbing.

Animals begin to gather, where the noise is not, where the blades are not, where Death is not.

Just when I thought they were upon me, the women broke for lunch—giving others the chance to arrive; I could smell the vinegar on the pickles and, afterwards, the many pipes and many more cigarettes. Their smoke blew across to me, crouched, as fresh-smelling as it ever is—as if it were indeed curative.

Now it is noon. Olwyn knows I am not where I should be.

Then my grandfather gave the shout, the combine started up and all barrels and sights turned towards where I lay.

I had never pretended to make a virtue of living like an animal, but now I was about to die like one. I was sport—accidental sport.

My thoughts were far from profound, entering what should have been the final five minutes of my life. I thought about the different kinds of pain that would be acceptable or not.

I can bear the idea of being dead but not the idea of being dead whilst wearing a dress of black silk.

Having witnessed, in the camp, the two day's death of a gutshot escapee, I knew I wanted it in the head. And God help now I was entirely trapped, pinned down, as were the animals around me.

Strangely, although I very much wanted to avoid dying, I did not want to do so at the price of surrender. I knew I would rather die, and die in agony, than face the kindnesses of surrender.

The badger was stepping on the rats as he ran from corner to corner of the remaining square; . . .

. . the rats were biting one another, biting anything that came within snap-range of their back-heading-teeth; . . .

. . the harvest mice trembled on the upper parts of the stems, as if they might climb out of trouble; . . .

. . the rabbits were the worst—I could almost hear them saying "Oh my! Oh my!" to one another as they clumped together in quivering mounds.

I felt bizarrely elated to be part of the collective again, even if it was the collective of fear—some of us would survive, not all of me would die.

Although at home everywhere, a gentleman has only one true home—the field of battle.

The rats were limbs, though, extra ones—when a bullet hit them, I felt pained.

Blood-flutters: The air is a soup of white chaff.

I was a rat trapped inside a human body trapped inside a human trap for rats.

The air was too packed with information-fear for me to be simply able to breathe it. The winnow of the wheat floated like a soup—as gelatine is to water, so the air was to usual air. The scorch was all around me of animal anger; their sense of injustice—their desire to obliterate whatever force it was that kept coming in fragments towards us.

Whenever one of the braver or more terrified animals tried to make a dash, they were gunned down within a few feet of the edge. Sometimes we could feel the light spray of their vital juices, a wet shower of bone fragments a few of which reached down to us through the wheat stalks.

Not crows, though.

I had one chance—to use my voice; to shout "Stop! Stop!" and slowly stand up, raising my hands: "Stop shooting! I am a man, not an animal! In here!

I surrender!" That was the scene that, if I wished to survive, I would have to play out.

No; never; rather die; rather let them find a curled-up, chopped-up corpse and realize their mistake.

The uncut wheat, as far as I can tell, is down to the size of a couple of tennis courts.

All around me was high squealing, like logs sometimes do when you put them sappy too sappy on the fire. Every animal in the corn square was now death-fearing. Some stood still and shivered. The new smell was of sweet rodent urine—a little like cornfield smell, but intensified. All these creatures had eaten and fertilized these crops for generations—and their aunts and uncles and nieces and nephews would continue to do so. But for us, it was time to die. I felt thirsty.

Then the rooks arrive because the rooks arrive.

There is confusion; those shooting do not know whether they should continue. But then, it seems, all the other animals decide this is the time to make a run for it. I see the badger go, drawing immediate fire. Two rabbits are gunned down within a couple of feet. The hare, which I didn't know was there before, streaks away out of sight. Rats swarm as one; some of them, also, will get through.

The rooks were the North, East, South and West Winds, all over and around me.

In the wing-fluster I close my eyes. The rooks are attacking me with their beaks.

One can only imagine what it looks like from the periphery of the cornfield; carrion-frenzy.

The black of their wings; the black of my dress: "It will keep you safe."

I am lifting off the ground and bumping back and lifting again; strings.

A gentleman should dress as if having received wardrobe advice from his man, his mistress, a meteorologist, and himself ten years into the future.

Gunshots continue.

The rooks' beaks take hold of the strings of the dress; I had wanted Olwyn to make me fly, now I must hold still.

I find my face in the belly of one bird, its claws grab my ears for purchase—it is blacking me out.

Noise the noise noise; tremolo.

Having an experience without having it; blindfold vision; high-wrapping. But I knew I was going upwards and upwards.

. . be patient.

I understand the need to eliminate rodents.

Isn't my weight too much for them? Won't they fail, and drop me back down, and splinter, and make off back to The Darkenings.

The blood of a rook, bullet-struck, sprays against my arm.

Because Olwyn made it, and she knows everything, the black silk must surely hold.

I feel I am now at a height where, if I were dropped I would certainly die.

The air was cooler; the noise didn't mean anything; bullets still whistled.

Why could I not have been changed into a flying animal? Or even a digging animal—a mole might have escaped.

I can imagine the thunder of the tractor and its many dragged wheeled blades as they rose and then fell above us. Dirt fell down, dried dirt, within the tunnel. With the increased sensitivity of my hearing, it was the end of the world. With mole-ears, it was the loudest, most terrifying sound I had ever heard. I dug down to one of the deeper tunnels, where the noise was still apocalyptic; the lower I got, the less I cared about the deaths of the other animals. If they couldn't come down here, they weren't worth life.

The bird on my face seemed to be shivering; I felt wetness run into my eye.

"Thank you," I said to the rooks.

All tunnels must stray a little if they are get us to our destination without collapse.

"Thank you," I said to Olwyn.

Education: The wisdom of animals bounces back off other animals; if it isn't emitted, it doesn't exist.

. . .

Beaks and claws have saved my life; burnished.

I am still on my back; even if I could see, I would see only the blue of the sky.

The treetops, as we descended into them, began to change the sounds I heard. I felt more accompanied.

I am expecting to be placed down on the ground, right in front of the hut. Instead, I feel leaves against my feet and elbows as the blackness begins to dissipate, as the feathers stop touching me.

We have come to rest in the treetops.

Again, a long way down.

The rook from my face falls into my lap. It has red blood on its breast. It seems to be looking at me, perhaps expecting me to kill it.

I cradle the rook.

When the rook dies, I will bury it.

. . .

Clamour from over towards the field, and then horses trotting through The Darkenings.

I am within sight of the hut; no-one looks up. I am thirsty.

My grandfather has come to check on Olwyn.

He walks in through the door, and comes out a couple of seconds later. I hear him say the word, "Nothing."

. . .

I bundled myself into an invisible ball, hid my eyes in the black silk. And so, I don't know if anyone glanced up at the rooks; I did my best to hide.

Their horses take them back to the slaughter.

. . .

When I was sure they were gone, I began to make my way to the ground.

Tree-climbing—I found it hard to believe this was once my greatest pleasure.

"Of course I was lying when I said about not being able to read," said Olwyn.

The witch smiles at you.

The dying rook seemed to become, with every moment, with every movement closer to the ground, heavier and heavier.

Let us address each other frankly, after all this time of evasion, I and I.

"I have read every sentence you have written," she said.

> When I laid it on the earth, just for a moment, so I could take a moment to recover, the black feathers became white flesh, the rook turned back into Olwyn.

She pauses for a moment, and yawns.

No, one absolutely can't—We are unable—I find it completely impossible to progress beyond this sentence, this word; which is not to be the last sentence in this set of notes but should be taken to be the last word before I depart. Hurried.

A gentleman must . . .

That skin is so pale! Her fore-arm.

> Olwyn who had been the rook was wounded, mortally. Here is where I notice she is bleeding.

She yawns until the blood comes into the back of her mouth.

Her wrist.

She was bleeding as a rook—and when she returned to human size, the wound grew with her.

This we have left for you, being plural, passing through, past and future tense, attempting to learn, failing, usually failing.

She saves me and dies.

"Delay, it's all been about delay."

What I was thinking is, "I should not have tried to go to the house this morning. This is my fault."

"Listen to me," she said.

I listen.

> I carried Olwyn into the house and laid her out on the bed . . .

"By trial and error I've found a route that keeps you here the longest."

Olwyn will explain how she has managed to keep you here so long: . . .

. . by blowing your parachute so it comes down in The Darkenings, . . .

. . by having you stick in the tree and then fall and twist your ankle (very often this goes wrong, and you die or are uninjured), . . .

. . by sewing shut your beautiful eyes, . . .

. . by letting you have your head, make what you think are mistakes, . . .

. . by keeping you as a tortoiseshell cat . . .

. . and as thirty-seven rats, . . .

. . by burying you alive, . . .

. . by letting you seduce her, . . .

. . by dressing you in black silk, . . .

. . and by this last.

Everything she has done, she says, is to extend if only by a few minutes the time she gets to spend with you.

"This is the way that keeps you here longest—it would take too long to explain why. I don't have much time. This time. If I don't let you go do each thing, at that particular moment, it all goes wrong.

 "If it's changed by even a minute, one way or the other, you get caught or killed earlier.

"I have to balance up your impatience and your fear.

"It has to be a mix of holding you back and letting you go.

"I can only keep you as a cat so long . . . I want to live with a man, not a cat.

"If I tell you too soon about the rounds, the returns, you try to burn down The House Beautiful.

"I like to keep you in your box of hate, you're very predictable that way.

"You won't believe you can't do what you want—even now you think you can trick your way through to success.

"Always, in the end, you are drawn to your futile mission at the house—just trying to see if this time you can trick your way through.

"I can't stop you going—so this is the best way.

"Dying, it's the only way to be sure I'll bring you back.

"You've been getting closer and closer to using the knife.

"I see you, at the last moment.

"I have to give you a reason not to want to do it.

"I am watching, when you go in.

"Do you understand? Are you listening?

"All of this, what I do, what I say, what I don't say—every single tiny detail is just to make you stay here a little longer."

Then I speak.

Speaking one's love to the object of one's obsession was like finally jumping out of the plane.

What shines there here also shines.

What I say seems to bring Olwyn that much closer to death. But she speaks, less articulately, more falteringly than I write it.

"Thank God.

"It's me dying that forces you to say it direct—otherwise you never actually get round to it. And oh how I need to hear it direct, out loud, so that I can keep myself going.

"Many's the time I've ended the whole thing in seconds.

"I go up and rip your parachute down the middle, watch you fall to the High Field with a thud. It seems kinder to us both.

"But because I know this can happen, with you speaking out—if I do everything in a certain way, just right—it makes the lives bearable.

"The other lives.

"Maybe if I keep going, I'll find a better way. Maybe I won't have to be so cruel to you.

"I promise, I'm going to try. But I've promised that before.

"You are such a headstrong man.

"Unless I die, you never say it. You go off without a word. I need to hear you say it, otherwise I can't keep on.

"You can't keep away from that blessed house, no more than blood can avoid the heart.

"This is the only way. At least I get to watch you sleep."

She pauses, for strength.

She tells you where to find your suit. It is beneath the mattress you have been sleeping on, the mattress upon which you have laid her down. It is all pressed flat, as if ironed.

She tells you where to find this book—this book containing these words in this handwriting, continuing beyond the end of the card-index.

I had to walk a certain number of paces this way, that way.

And there it is, concealed in a hole at the bottom of a tree, wrapped in oilcloth.

You will carry it back to her, put it in her white hands.

She will hand the package back to me with a sombre, sober expression, then laugh.

"I enjoyed it this time," she will say. "This time was a good one—the best."

I unwrap the oilcloth and find these notes; this book.

It has a cover of black leather and pages of soft white paper. This book—the book.

The writing—your handwriting—is in ink and pencil.

"What do they say?" is what I ask.

She answers, as she has before.

"You have time to read them," she said.

Until you have read this through, do not write in it. If you choose to do so, that is your own mistake.

"Why didn't you give this to me before?"

This book; these notes.

Her white skin begins to sink into her white bones.

One knew that on certain days one would not be able to recognize her.

This was beauty, to see the mouse within her face become the skeleton of itself.

I recall my mother in the twilight in the twilight of my mother.

"How long before you die?" I ask.

The blankets are damson with blood.

"Moments," she said.

And "I will love you for ever" meets "I will always fall in love with you."

You speak.

These notes in this book are something different.

You ask her not to let you have the book until after she has been mortally wounded.

You say you want things to go exactly as they have, if that is what she wants.

You promise crying to try to resurrect her.

You promise crying to resurrect her.

> Different—these notes—from the notes in the card-
> index.

She said, "You . . .

"You will—you always do."

> The card-index is the rough version; these notes, I see,
> these notes here in this book, are the whole story.

"However frustrating living is, I do much prefer it to
being dead."

I would I believe trade half my vocabulary to regain the
lost eloquence of my cat-tail—

> This book must be a record of my spiritual progress.

> If all this has happened before, why does it feel so
> freshly painful? If this is happening for the first time,
> why do I seem to know it so agonizingly well?

Death has an inhuman facility.

> To begin with, this book must have been empty—I must
> not have known where to begin. I expect I must have
> begun with an instruction to myself, to go to the card-
> index and begin work.

> If I can't explain it, it may be because I am inside it; all a-
> scribble.

Olwyn dies.

From this time, I work.

Only the need to write this book could have brought
me to writing; I have no memories of ever previously
having rearranged words for my own displeasure.

Then you lay her out upon the card-index; some blood
seeps through, no matter.

You read for hours, then write for hours, every sentence
here, beside her corpse; beside her corpse, every sentence here.

She wished to preserve me but wished also to punish
me; this past tense is false. If she was and will be then
surely she is.

It says here that I love Olwyn in a way I had not realized
until I read it written down.

For a moment—glue—behind the nib the black ink
shines on the white page, then it dries and is sucked
down and all goes respectable. When one is fast there is
perhaps an inch of gloss behind one—then miles of
matt. For a moment after writing, it's like dawn hitting
the leading edge of the earth.

There is no reason why my handwriting should begin to
look like my grandfather's, particularly as I cannot
remember my grandfather's handwriting.

It's all in the same pen, but sometimes my hand is slant
and spiky, sometimes mellifluous, sometimes the ink
rains as if the nib hadn't touched the page.

If one were to dig, one knows one would only reach down as far as the layer of buried nibs.

One sentence a day, might that be possible? What would the time of the writing be then? And what could this possibly matter?

Grey-green mould fuzzing up the punctuation marks except ; this is blackened.

Using the card-index is the creation of work—work must be created to fill the time, to make the time exist for the future.

Very tense.

Before she dies, the last thing Olwyn says to me is that she wishes all this was all over.

I put the cards on the floor, in war-clouds, then rearrange them to make them better.

This is your experience—this is the scope of your experience—all that is left is for you to work on your memory. If one day, you can get a message to yourself to experience things more minutely, that would be useful. As it is, we are relying on the memories of an insufficiently attentive man.

Jack's a dull boy who can't remember a time he wasn't dull.

Everything eternally happens initially.

Some of these sentences were written a hundred or a thousand rounds before others of these sentences. One must be reasonably happy with whichever of them one has left unchanged. The book is the only thing we are aware of which does change, otherwise it could not have come to be written. Unless that, too, is an illusion—which is more probable than possible. So there is always hope that, one future round, through the agony of the book, through the agency of the book, some breakout will occur. We do not really believe in this, although I have hopes.

There have, I admit, been omittings, forgettings. You know of some moments too determinedly exquisite to be noted; many involving the moon and how it made Olwyn young again while it was young. Perhaps we have valued our own surprise more highly than we realize. One might as well exchange a perfectly predictable life for immediate death. Olwyn reads the card-index sentences; beloving. The dark of the evening around me smells almost Autumnal.

I spend some time with my knife, getting the dirt out from under my nails.

A whole section cannot be dedicated to regret as one was dedicated to clothes or eyelid sights. It can be dedicated to mourning, which is regretful. Regret is not wholehearted; it reserves the right to look constantly outwards.

My knife might as well have been hanging up all this time in a hunting lodge.

Sometimes he is my father, sometimes my grandfather, sometimes both—it seems to make no difference. He is my object, my grandfather, whatever year this is.

To the house: to the library: to the end: to here.

What is the difference between this time round and the last? Only these notes. These notes are slightly different, because I am adding to them now, this latest amendment. And because before I leave I may potentially add more to them—though I doubt it.

Swimming through frogs.

If I can learn from the notes then perhaps I can change what happens to me. That must be the hope.

Reference here to absolutely no hope.

To deny the existence of something so absolutely is to invite it round for supper.

Trying to achieve anything in these rounds is like trying to make a cake out of spaghetti.

If one were to exclude everything but Beauty, one might—moon, Olwyn, house, green—finish up with a wonderfully acceptable artefact; no audience.

Quite frankly, I am hungry enough to settle for either the spaghetti or the cake.

How far away the applause seems, as if it were for someone else altogether.

I have been thinking, (at this comma I gave up, I just gave up).

How humiliating to find that what one has been writing is a simple love letter, yet how wonderful.

My remarks here are remarks about the process of writing these remarks. Perhaps I should rephrase that— What else can these remarks be about but the process whereby these remarks came to be written? You're just going to have to live with that fact, as I'm living with that fact. Forgive me. I forgive you. Thank you. Don't mention it.

I have been thinking, (at this comma I became a chimpanzee and became hysterical).

The truth is of no benefit to a sentence; love is.

The undersides of the nettle-leaves looked as if they had been coated in milk, left to dry, and then veiled in spiderweb.

Less describing; more despairing.

Let it be unknown, and let it remain unknowable.

The mouth is of no benefit to a sentence.

A gentleman should have as deep a familiarity with the great religious texts of the world as is commensurable with not having read them.

Many more people than myself, I expect, I suspect, exist in a loop of recurring time; not eternal return, just circumscribed return—that one same thing over and over.

My blindnesses: I hear scissors, by mistake.

The questions now are, Do I want never to see The Darkenings again? Never to meet Olywn? Never to

suffer being held still? Never delight in being transformed? Never be chased? Never realize again the
identical, everlasting love? Never fail at murder?

Who knows what new free-fall would meet me, should I
succeed in breaking the cycle of rounds?

The ultimate choice, in the penultimate moment, has
always been left to me.

I am glad I get another chance to drink that cup of
water—perhaps next time I shall do it more graciously.

The King has acquired a King, for practice.

House, porous; Not like someone's imagination.

I have thought through the whole episode, start to
finish; I have had time—but to think through is not the
same as to begin to understand.

This is a day I am not sure I can remember.

It's a wise man who refrains from refraining.

I am remembering another life, one that involved quite
a lot of being rained on and not knowing where one
was.

Do you wish the world—as if across the playground—
would run away from you—as if you were It?

Nothing is created or destroyed, but something is
changed. The card-index is shuffled. The book is copied

out. I learn different things every time, from what I have written before.

What happens to the rest of the black silk?

If I succeed in killing either Churchill or my grandfather, I may escape from the rounds—something I no longer wish to do. And so, what I intend is to see that I can do it, if I wish: I must get close enough to be able to rehearse the kill I will one day make. This, perhaps, is not entirely true. Perhaps it is what an assassin needs to say to himself. Perhaps it is what a traitor needs to say to himself.

What shines here shines also there.

I wore the trousers with braces, but not the jacket; I would not put on the jacket until I went to kill my grandfather; fate.

Look, the decision-monster, riding through its own crimson!

Here are occurrences only, not and never events— events are a necessary humanization of the universe; the illusion we need in order to move our hand a single millimetre.

Unable, unable.

If I aim to bring this corpse my love back to life, I must die and then hate her.

Unblackened.

There is hardly time to read all this: a day before tonight. How did I find time to write it? A year of days.

It is hard to think of unprecedented things whilst seated beside the dead body of . . .

Almost infinite time to test the limits of a very limited sensibility; fast.

Sometimes what one writes is exactly what someone else would have wanted to say.

This atrocious sadness and these immanent burdens.

I still have no idea what she has done for me. Has she died in order to force me to return her to life? Or is it, instead, more of an invitation? We both may return— almost certainly will—but for how long will we be dead? For how long will we be apart? How much of this did she know? How much of this did she force?

One reluctantly accepts one's inevitable triumph.

If this is happening for the first time, why do I seem to know it so agonizingly well? If all this has happened before, why does it feel so freshly painful?

You will be grateful that you asked Olywn to hide this book, when she returns and finds it, because you will be able to experience the whole thing again for the first time. Blessing.

<u>My love, memorize this:</u> Written in not my own handwriting, and all underlined.

There are no consequences; no consequences as such.

If it is to remain comprehensible, this book must per-petually climb out of itself.

Nothing could be achieved by sentences beginning with Nothing—or ending, Nothing.

How long does it take for bubbles to appear in a glass of water? Do you know? You must know, because I know, and I know already.

An evening, green.

By this time, I have stopped crying in pain and frustration.

The ultimate choice, in the ultimate moment, has always been mine. (We are not sure it is accurate to call it choice; it is something much more like your sweet doom.)

All it takes is one time for my knife to do my thinking for me.

The decision-monster: Perhaps you will decide to return to the woman you only discovered you loved a few hours ago, in order to spend most of your time with her hating and resenting her. Crimson.

This is where you read what Olwyn has written down for you.

I can't have started writing in this book until I was sure what I had was perfect; near-perfect. I am my own scribe.

It is like looking back at a mediaeval self: lost years of copying; I can't correct this—this must be the most I can say, apart from the final entry.

It is finished, all that remains is the copying. I have time—I have more than more than enough time.

I will leave myself a note or two.

> Exactly follow these instructions in order to get to the library.

The bomb is coming down—I am the bomb—the bomb has not yet been dropped—I cannot prevent myself. I would not now prevent myself, even if I could.

Olwyn doesn't forget. Olwyn knows. She has learnt what to do, over the course of an infinite number of visits. Her anger at me is real; she wishes she could do something different than sew my eyes together. Of course, she has read the book. Olwyn is reading this.

> Once you are in the library, you are on your own.

This has long ago ceased to be about anything other than being human.

I miss Christmas as I miss all the other annuals— frogspawn and pancakes with lemon and sugar, snow- drops and snowfall and hard nutty nougat, hares on the hillside and fresh nettle-stings.

> Be ready to set off from my house at half past seven in the evening, by the church bells; do not set off, though, for at least another fifteen minutes.

> Take a final look around, at the place, at me, laid out there. I am not as dead as I look—I wish that I were—I am quite capable of coming with you.

My hating her will be my loving her.

> Around twenty-five to eight, you will hear a sound outside, very like a gunshot. Ignore this. It is a motorbike dispatch rider leaving the house, taking an important Prime Ministerial message to London.

> At this point, put on the jacket of your suit.

A gentleman should never quote anyone but his nanny, and then only back at her, with fondness, just before she dies.

> Set fire to the cottage with me inside it. I have left some petrol for you, in a can behind the stove.

> This will draw some of the men from the house. With the dry August weather, they fear a forest fire.

> Do not worry about the damage. Nothing matters now. You're not able to destroy it unless you're able to destroy everything.

> Wait until it is good and caught. The card-index burns particularly well.

Her hating me will be her loving me.

At 8 p.m., we should be at the edge of The Darkenings, on the edge of the field, facing the house, staying out of sight behind a tree.

Wait until the church bells chime the hour before doing anything. This is the most important timing.

I will not say try not to be impatient, that is what you are, but try not to act on your impatience immediately. Believe me, when you've done this, it has not helped.

If you feel you are being watched, do not worry, that is me, I am watching you.

You cannot see me, so there's no point looking around, but I know you will.

Now they have harvested it, the cornfield offers no cover.

You must skirt the hedgerow, head down, loping.

Turn right and go anti-clockwise to avoid the military policemen, Harold and Ben, sitting on their motorbikes at the left edge of the field, discussing football.

Harold will notice the fire in The Darkenings at a quarter past eight.

Before she died, the last thing Olwyn said to me was that she wished all this was all over.

If you move as soon as Harold and Ben start to run, that is your timing. Go earlier and one of the military police,

Simon, will spot you as he sprints across the field. Go later, Gaiters will walk almost right over you.

And do not be tempted to take this book with you. Leave it in the cottage to burn.

It is quite dark, with the moon covered by clouds, and you will not be easy to spot against the hedge. The men will be too excited, running towards the fire, organizing one another.

You will see the patch of unscythed corn in the middle of the field.

Be careful but not timid.

At 8.22 p.m., arrive at the bottom of the garden.

Wait until Gaiters comes out of the house and crosses to the kennels, to feed the hounds, at 8.24 p.m.

Gaiters glances once towards the wheatfield, when he is ten paces from the house—make sure you are ducking down behind the privet at this point.

Thanks to your previous exploits, everyone is on the look-out.

Gaiters spots the smoke rising above The Darkenings just at the moment when Harold rushes back out shouting fire!

Gaiters begins to walk with his limp across the field, to see what Harold means.

Now is your chance, but you have only a few seconds.

Run straight up the garden, as far as the fifth bush—the rabbit.

(A gentleman should never run, except towards certain death.)

Climb up inside the bush, just as you did before.

Wait.

Breathe as quietly as you can.

Seven people run past. Count them.

When the last is gone, you will have two minutes to get into the house. Do not make any detours.

You need not be too careful here—until a maid looks out of a downstairs window, no-one's glance passes over the garden.

There are two armed men, military police, patrolling the hall. If they capture you before you reach the library, you will not get a chance to come near your father; they will dispose of you before you've even had the chance to address one word to him.

You will set off full of the right intentions, it is only towards the very end that you begin to weaken. There must be some escape from these rounds, and perhaps this is the time you will trick your way through, our way out. But the fact you are reading these words, again, shows that you failed the last time, and every previous time. Perhaps it would be better were you to read no further. Perhaps it would be better if you tried to attempt something outrageously unprecedented.

At 8.29 p.m. one of the military police will go to the library to check on Churchill; the other will go to the kitchen to fetch a glass of milk. This is your chance. Go into the hall, go into the secret passage.

Once you are inside the walls, you are safe from discovery. Make sure the panel is securely fastened behind you.

I will have gone to the kennels, to release the hounds.

At half past eight, the grandmother clock strikes in the hall, and a minute later, the grandfather clock strikes in the upstairs hall. You must move as soon as you hear the grandfather.

You must use the secret passage from the master bedroom to the library. This is why they chose you for this. No-one else would be able to get anywhere near.

Your father and Churchill will be alone, in club chairs, before the fire—this must have been the picture you had.

In fact, you cannot tell from behind whether it is your father or your grandfather—and you have always known it makes no difference. Kill one, kill both.

Emerge into the library just after Churchill says, "Latterly . . ."

(A gentleman should enter the room as if he had not existed before, and depart in the manner of an eternal verity.)

You will be over-awed by Churchill just as you were overawed by Hitler. These are the two opposite ends of the round, unless you count the parachute jumps—the moment you fall into the skies, that is the beginning.

You will stand there, knife to his throat, and if you are only able to kill him then all this will surely have to be different.

If for once you are able to do something different . . . If for once you are able to cut. Please, kill him.

But so far, you have not, and so other things happen.

This must be what happens, because nothing else could bring you back to here.

The library begins to purr, as if you were all inside the voicebox of a lion. The sound so low you feel it before you hear it.

At first you think an earthquake is happening.

The vibration of the floor travelling up through my legs begins to give me pins and needles.

(There is no other way of describing pins and needles, except perhaps as the purr of a non-existent cat within one's body.)

The spines of the books become lumpy with rivets.

The library is suddenly filled with the baying of the hounds.

A gun touches you and you are afraid.

(A gentleman should die with an air of mild curiosity.)

A gun touches your right temple.

"If you try to escape, you will be shot." It is Gaiters.

(A gentleman should greet with genuine warmth only the following persons: his sister's daughters, his maternal aunts and his mortal enemies.)

As you stand paralysed, Winston Churchill moves a small Chippendale table and then the military policemen begin to roll back the Afghan rug, their feet juddering against the floor.

A trapdoor will be revealed. The two halves of it open downwards, a long slit down the middle of a coffin-shape.

You will not try to escape and so you will not be shot.

You are led to the bomb doors, for this is what they are, . . .

. . Winston Churchill to your left, . . .

. . your father to your right.

We look through the bomb doors of the library, through the smoke of the flak, and see far beneath us the vast darknesses of Germany.

A parachute is placed on your back (you have ceased resisting)—the straps are tightened after the harness is clicked into place.

Churchill will address you, "For England," he will say.

"For myself and for Olwyn," you will reply.

"As if there is a difference," Churchill will reply, amused.

"I could have killed Hitler," you say.

Churchill replies, "I am extremely obliged to you for not doing so."

Churchill will pass you a cigarette and then light it for you.

(A gentleman should smoke, if not for personal pleasure then to set his companions at their ease.)

Everything initially happens eternally.

Churchill says, "We have both dabbled with forces we little comprehend."

He pauses, then continues, "For this, no doubt, we shall be made to suffer."

You smoke your cigarette.

He smokes his cigarette. The cigar is for the public.

He asks if you are ready?

You say you are ready.

You realize you haven't said anything to your father.

You say, "Next time."

Just then, I turn the handle and let the hounds into the room.

Eternal cat, eternal rat, eternal blindness, eternal falling—you have a series of eternities to look forward to and to remember.

You are pushed from behind through a large, loud hole in the floor; coffin-sized.

(A gentleman should have only one proper relation to force, whether suffered or exerted, and that is noncha-lance.)

Four of the younger, more eager hounds fall with you, and when you pull the cord on your parachute you watch them dropping away from you, evaporating before they get anywhere near hitting the ground. (I have made this up. I have no way of knowing this hap-pens. But I do see some hounds go with you. Maybe they do not evaporate, maybe they disappear in another way. But I can see them falling, so they exist beyond the point of the bomb doors.)

You fall towards Germany.

You will be free at every point to do exactly as you have always—gnaw—done.

The moment you are out of the bomb doors, you will remember nothing of any of this; this is the time at which time restarts.

It is not that you forget, it must be that it has not yet happened.

In this you may take comfort: There are many parts of many lives which are worse.

But do what they ask you to do. Try, somehow, to remember this.

It doesn't make any difference, I am sure, but I have to know that I have written it.

There is, I feel, a very good chance that this is heaven.

There are cycles within cycles: bed to bed, tree to tree, plane to plane, word to word.

If and when you fail with Churchill, you must remember to go along with everything Hitler asks. Unless you do this, you will never see me again.

When you think about it, it's no stranger, and a lot more efficient, than any supposedly normal human existence. We—Olwyn and I—are merely caught up in a tighter loop of time, and one that cuts out the labour of growing up.

One can't keep past, present and future distinct— because they're not.

I will be waiting for you.

Remember: ignorance.

And, no, Olwyn never writes anything but the instructions in the book. We believe she has her own far superior book.

I have just now spent half a day looking for Olwyn's book, but I couldn't find it.

Good advice is always worthwhile, even if the time when might act upon it is long gone or is never to come.

> And now I will put this where you can find it, when you need it, in the tree, then fly to rescue you, as rooks.

July for Germany; August for England. The Western half of the infinite.

This is not death as death.

Your loss becomes your gift.

You will be grateful that you asked Olywn to hide the book, because you will be able to experience the whole thing again for the first time. Blessing.

It was she who forced me to do it; she made everything that happened happen. Because she knew the world would reset, and she would have me back again.

This is not what I hold to be true, only my own particular flavour of inarticulacy.

In England I was the corpse, in Germany I am the grave-digger.

The truth cannot be fitted inside a sentence—it is too simple for that.

To become perfect—this is contradictory. If something had to become perfect then, at some stage, it was less than perfect—and to be truly perfect a perfect thing must always have been perfect.

(A gentleman shall continue to be a gentleman in whatever circumstances he may find himself.)

I've done everything right, which is why I've made nothing but mistakes.

Particular: There is a wisdom-surplus.

Might there be, do you perhaps think, something you should not have invented?

When I say I have given up entirely, what I means is— the world has the consistency of overboiled cabbage. Crowd-master.

Only imbalance and ineptitude are beloved; as onlookers, we are all toddler-mummies.

If this were simply a repetition, one would have known. Instead, beneath me I saw exactly what I expected to see; Soon.

Something truly violent can only happen over a matter of years; decapitation is as nothing when compared with disillusion.

One day I shall find a way to squeeze out all the pus that's inside me into a series of buckets.

The only things worth doing are the things that cannot be done.

The only wisdom to be gained from experiences is to avoid believing in one's own wisdom.

Less of more.

A thousand years of weeks and weeks—Riot!—of graphite.

As long as the hero is bang in the centre of the big screen, there is the chance at something beyond heroism.

A sound in my head, the universe tumbling downstairs.

Knowing what one wants to have done is a far simpler thing than knowing what one wants to do.

It is not that I forget, it is that it hasn't yet happened to be rememberable.

I looked out of the window of my imaginary train, running where no tracks run, and saw myself waving joyfully from one of those woods-which-disappear-too-fast, those places I had always grieved I would never reach.

One knew one could have been happy, placed only in this place, being only with this being, and so one knew one had to flee.

A totally predictable life; an immediate death: same difference.

It is green evening, my friend, and getting close to the time to burn the house.

No Greeks or Trojans, only my grandfather and myself.

It was no longer the mission, it was the need to reject everything that wasn't the mission.

For the life I have been forced to lead I blame the people that I never chanced to meet.

An extremely abnormal but yet human perspective.

Beware yourself!

I will go soon, returning across the cut cornfield—I will pad back, hard feet on hard-packed earth, like a cat or a fox returning.

Annihilate regret and you'll regret it.

A gentleman, having once departed, should never return.

If I can ever do better in the past, I am doing it.

Always judge midway through; the end is absolutely the wrong time for any kind of summation.

If I could change the future, I would have done it already.

Know that the only journey you will ever be able to take isn't over the hills and far away but around the houses.

One doesn't believe one has degenerated from an earlier ideal; instead, one is maturing into a decadence one has desired from the beginning.

Never the long-warm-shadowed days of Autumn, never the long-cold-shadowed days of January.

A pair of binoculars, dangling by their leather strap from the highest branch of an oak tree; a familiar world.

Swimming through myself.

I am not smoking as I write this, and not wearing a false moustache and beard.

I recall my mother in the twilight and I recall the twi-light in my mother.

Death was an inhuman facility.

I could die this very moment, but I won't, but I could, but I won't, but I could.

Seated at the Captain's table, the Ship of Fools, the morning of April 1st.

There are compensations, but then one has to be stupid enough to enjoy them.

I am pricked by heavens.

Don't worry, it has only taken an aeon to achieve this ignorance.

There are twisted things, dripping with effluent, infinitely malevolent, just out of sight—in whichever direction one stares, one will miss them. Happy Birthday.

There is no reason not to.

I write this at a certain point, about to go into action. I re-write it from what I can remember of last time. I remember a little more each time; ground-time.

Because I remain human, I continue to think—perhaps this time, perhaps this time.

I, the bull-headed, am charging repeatedly into the hard wall of the limestone cliff because, so I once heard, there is beyond it a wide valley, and, on the far side of that valley, a beautiful limestone cliff.

I wish every ignorant instant of my life with Olwyn to be exactly the same. Style is the future rewriting itself.

Birth-pangs; growing-pains; death-throes—avoid the whole kit and.

Admissions of weakness come from positions of strength.

I would I believe trade half my vocabulary to regain the lost eloquence of my cat-tail—

Put the cardboard with the cardboard; keep the glitter against the flesh.

Air-thrum: At moments you are known to have applauded.

"Which side are you on, finally?" "I am against myself."

It's where you are utterly certain I would never go that you should seek me first.

I am not sentimental about this, I hope; I would wish us both dead, if we could be cleanly and permanently so—and our bodies interred side by side. No, I am not in any way at all sentimental about this.

Tumbling thoughts, that I can assure myself I will not have.

I should really find another name for my knife.

To escape oneself: The things, the acts, such impossibilities of language have been allowed. It is only through these sense-lesions that we pass succulently into life. There has to be, behind the wound, a yearning to turn communication into communion—if there is that, if that isn't there, all is pure avoidance. I want you to know—I need you to know—there is value beyond desire for display.

It's as if the poor man's been falling to bloody bits all the time, at every single one of these moments, and all I've done is watch.

I don't believe in anything I've written. How can one?
(This is the only way to be trustworthy.) Who is going
to vouch for such and such? A plaint; avowed.

How the poor chap wishes he could speak to Olwyn,
one last little time before the next time. What he would
say to her . . . How she would react . . . And he is saying,
and she is reacting, and we are just watching.

For long long hours, or so they seemed at the time, I
lolled on her lap, cat-head slowly bouncing upon the
tump of her tummy, bathing in her breath, listening to
the lull of her song.

"Tell me about the cards," I say. "Whose are they? Who
wrote on them?"

And still I can do nothing but look forward to my next
set of mournings.

If one can one does, doesn't one? One simply can't stop
oneself.

So sorrowed of the time and lonely of this world.

What shines there here also shines.

Too early or too late, everything. Smudge. Yet once one
fully accepts it, the time—it seems—fully redeems itself.

My existences are either without irony or are nothing
but, depending upon how they are viewed; not by
myself.

Irony is the coup de grâce of self-defeat.

Horses are there to be ridden; men to be fooled.

Trust horses and dogs; gingerly.

A gentleman, having once departed, should never return.

Analogue; I will be aware it is thither I go; I will know it is hither I shall be returning; I do not need to be convinced I am to forget all of this, blankly—but for now I remember it—for a few lines more, before I walk outside.

What is this if not a *lyrisches* poem? Native, unstolen land.

Remember ignorance.

This world desperately is too full of worlds abstractly for one person beautifully to dwell in it comprehensively.

Said the man to the tree; extravagant.

One hopes finally one will be seen as having behaved in
a gentlemanly fashion, despite the circumstances having
been somewhat trying.

And in this breathed breath, so death is undeathed.